TO SMOKE

ELISE FABER

TO SMOKE
by Elise Faber

Copyright © 2021 ELISE FABER
Newsletter sign-up

TO SMOKE
Copyright © 2021 ELISE FABER
Print ISBN: 978-1-63749-007-5
eBook ISBN: 978-1-63749-006-8
Cover Art by Jena Brignola

SMOKE

IT CHOKES.

It obscures.

It burns the eyes and the throat, and sometimes, even the skin.

But sometimes where there's smoke, there's fire.

And sometimes that hidden fire is where the most sacred of treasures are hidden.

CHAPTER ONE

Darcy

CREAM SAUCE SHOULD GO to hell.

Or at least, cream sauce that hadn't been watched carefully enough and left to burn, scalding itself on the bottom of the pan and creating an impenetrable layer of burnt butter, flour, and milk that she was now attempting to remove...*that* type of cream sauce could go to hell.

And if *she* was supposed to have been the one watching said sauce while the head chef, Lex, had stepped out for a couple of minutes...then she supposed she could go to hell, too.

Oh, wait.

She forgot.

She was there already.

Good attitude, pumpkin.

Sighing—and deliberately pushing the memory of her mom's slightly disapproving chiding out of her mind because she didn't need something else that made her feel like shit—Darcy set down the pan she was scrubbing and rested her chin on her chest, her arms aching.

Obviously, it was her turn in the kitchen.

Obviously, she wasn't great at it, even though she truly didn't mind being there. It was just...hard to pay attention to *all* the things at once. No sooner had the timer dinged on the oven for the bread to be removed than the pasta water had boiled over. And then add in the sauce, one of the littles coming into the kitchen to beg a cookie, and...well, failure.

Not that failure was a new thing for her.

She...left a lot to be desired, and she knew it.

As an intermediate soldier, she only spent part of her time on patrols and actively protecting her people. The rest was passed here in the kitchen under Lex's tutelage or in the armory, resetting targets, oiling guns, making sure the light bulbs were replaced. She did time with the kids during their lessons, helping them with the basics of elemental magic, encouraging them to learn control.

Thankfully, she'd moved up from toilet scrubbing and base-board dusting—and the dreaded maintenance of the flower beds.

Her elemental specialty was fire.

Her secondary specialty was telekinesis.

She didn't *do* plants, and any time she attempted to use the trickle of earth magic she possessed to help them grow or, hell, tried to *weed* the garden, she ended up with ash where once there had been lush greenery.

Moving her from a junior to an intermediate soldier had really been an attempt to save the gardens.

And she couldn't be mad at it, not with the evidence of ash around her.

So needless to say, Darcy didn't mind her time in the kitchen. Fire was much more akin to food and cooking, even though Lex preferred good old hard work to magic in this instance, she didn't mind that either. It felt good to use her hands, her muscles, to give her mind and all the trapdoors and landmines within it a break.

She didn't even mind the orders he lobbed at her that had

her running around like a chicken sans head, or the pot scrubbing and dish washing that seemed to go on forever at the end of her shift.

Because cooking—and cleaning—reminded her of her mom, and Darcy missed her, and the orders . . . well, they reminded her of her mom as well.

A grin curved her lips before she got back to scrubbing.

Her mom's orders were the reason she was a good soldier.

Ha.

Not so much. Less good soldier and more...problem with authority.

She knew she had a chip on her shoulder a mile wide, knew she questioned the orders given her far too often—though she *had* gotten better at the timing of said questions (read: doing them privately and preferably, not in the heat of the moment), but there was a reason her peers had achieved senior soldier status while she hadn't as of yet.

Orders. Her resistance to them. Her questioning them.

Not ideal when the entire system relied on a chain of command. It was just...what if the orders *weren't* the right ones in the pressure cooker of a situation? Her mother was gone, was dead because of a breakdown in the system, because someone hadn't thought through all the angles, and that had left her family unprotected.

Who could blame Darcy for wanting to make sure things were done correctly? That everyone, even those who were on the fringes, were remembered?

No one.

That was who.

Of course, that questioning wasn't conducive to a promotion.

Sighing, she dumped out the water, squirted in some more soap and fresh water, and went back to scrubbing.

Because in the grand scheme of things, she wasn't in any hurry.

She preferred things on her own timeframe, and since the extended life of a Rengalla meant that she might well live many more centuries, truly, what *was* the hurry?

Or at least, that was what she told herself.

Because the truth was that she was getting a bit...tetchy.

The knock on the counter made her jump, her hands splashing water from the basin and soaking her front.

She narrowed her eyes, glared at the intruder.

Not that it would matter.

Morgan never cared that he'd annoyed her.

Nope. The man lived to press her buttons, to infuriate. Ever since—

And she wasn't going to cross that particular mental mine-field. No freaking way.

"Earth to Darcy," he said, mouth curving into a careless smile. "Are you mooning over the latest boy band? Or maybe dreaming of whether your last name will be Carter or Timber-lake?" He tapped his lips. "Oh! Or maybe you've gone modern, and it will be Styles."

"Ugh," she muttered, not just because she was a rock 'n' roll girl, but because she had got caught dancing to a poppy song one time—*one* time!—and the years of teasing certainly weren't worth the catchy chorus. She picked up the next pot. "What do you want?"

He shrugged, a lazy raise of one broadly muscled shoulder. "To torment you."

She rolled her eyes. "Well, luckily, I'm familiar enough with that course of action. I don't need any more." A flick of her hand to the door—and oops—she might have flung water and suds *accidentally* in his direction. So clumsy, she was.

He laughed, the sound sliding down her spine like honey as he grabbed a dish towel and wiped off the mess she'd made of his simple black tee. Simple being a poor description. Yeah, it was plain. Yeah, it was just black cotton. But hell no was it simple, not when it was Morgan filling out the material. The man had always been too gorgeous for words and too dangerous for her self-control.

"What do you want?" she snapped, going back to the cream sauce and finally—*finally!*—making progress of the scalded mess on the bottom of the pot.

Another shrug as he picked up some dishes she'd already cleaned and left to dry on the rack and began wiping them down. Then he did the next one.

And the next.

The man was being helpful.

Which immediately made her suspicious.

When he glanced up at her, one eyebrow lifted. She mentally shook herself and continued washing the pot. Eventually, the cream sauce submitted in its final battle, and she continued cleaning the remainder of the utensils, dishes, and pots and pans.

Scrub. Rinse. Put on the dish rack. Ignoring that Morgan was still there, still helping her by drying and putting everything away.

Disregarding his presence—or pretending to, anyway—she kept working until her job was done.

And *still*, he didn't say anything.

Well, that was fine. She didn't have to say anything either. Everything that needed to be said between them had been said. Years ago. If he wanted to languish his time away in the kitchens, that was fine by her.

For now, she had finished what she needed to get done. So, she would hang up her apron, get the fuck out of there. Because *she* was tired, and *she* was leaving. Regardless of whatever the annoying man still holding the dish towel had to say about it.

Unfortunately, he set down the towel and followed her out into the hall.

"Morgan," she said on a sigh, head falling back, eyes grazing the beautiful, magical murals that coated the walls.

He chuckled. "If I had a penny for every time I heard that

tone, that *sigh*"—he brought his fingers to his mouth in his version of a chef's kiss—"I'd be..." He trailed off, waggled his brows at her.

Darcy rolled her eyes but didn't bite.

Morgan continued walking by her side, weaving through the quiet corridors of the Colony. It was late, well after dinner service, and most people were back in their rooms.

But not her.

And not Morgan, who dogged her every step.

Until they finally reached her quarters.

She stopped in front of her door, plunked her hands on her hips, and glared at him. "I'm tired, and I don't have time for your bullshit."

Normally, he would have laughed again, would have made a snarky comment.

But instead, he smiled at her, his gorgeous hazel eyes soft and intense, and she felt a bolt of electricity shoot through her.

What? What the fuck was that? Had he just tried to unleash the Power of Hazel on her?

It wasn't going to work. She wasn't stupid. She—

Didn't get any further than that because he ran the backs of his knuckles over her cheek, stepped close. "I know you don't, Pem," he murmured, making her frown at the name. He'd never called her that before, even when—

She shook her head, pushed the memory of their failed weeklong relationship (yes, only a fucking *week!*) out of her brain, and opened her mouth to tell him to fuck right off.

He beat her by replying, "But you should know that I'll always have time for yours."

He had time for her bullshit? *Hers?* Laughter bubbled up in her throat. Was he fucking kidding? He'd gotten one glimpse— exactly *one* glimpse of her shit, and he'd dropped her faster than one of the scalding hot pots in Lex's kitchen. "I—"

"This is for you."

He shoved an envelope into her hands.

"What—?" Confusion warred with anger.

Before she could formulate a response, he was gone, long legs eating up the hall, disappearing around the corner. Shaken, she unlocked her door, moved inside her room, and collapsed onto the bed, where she opened the envelope.

And felt the bottom drop out of her world.

CHAPTER TWO

Morgan

HE FROWNED when he glanced up from the tablet screen that was displaying the roster for the perimeter shifts and didn't see a certain brown-eyed she-devil demanding to be debriefed on the coverage, triple-checking a system that had already been double-checked.

Darcy might be a handful and a half, but she was always on time.

And no one could truly fault her for wanting to make sure her fellow Rengalla were safe.

Not after what had happened to her family.

But maybe Dante had gone too easy on her in the beginning, had allowed her slack he wouldn't have given the other junior soldiers, promoted her even though her attitude had proved she wasn't ready for the responsibility.

So, they'd ended up with a monster of an intermediate soldier.

And…he'd—

Shaking his head, he glanced one more time at the tablet, at the shift assignments, and then at the space in front of him, as if that might have Darcy teleporting directly there.

The problem with that being...she couldn't teleport—only he and his two brothers could currently do that, though some of the kids working on their secondary magic skills showed some promise in that department. Another problem being that the shield made of Bond Magic that surrounded and protected and kept their home base—the Colony—from being discovered by prying eyes, prevented anyone from teleporting in and out of it.

He was currently out of it, as were all the other intermediate soldiers who were on patrol that day, as they were discussing expanding the shield to encompass more space.

Months ago, the shield had needed to be shrunk. With only Daughtry and Cody having the Bond Magic that was needed for the barrier, they couldn't maintain something so vast. But with the addition of Alex and John, Suz and Graham, his brother Mason and Gabby, now their proverbial cups runneth over with Bond Magic.

So...expanding.

So...additional soldiers for patrol today in order to make sure certain things were safe.

Their enemy had been vanquished in a big battle all those months before, when the shield had been erected, when Daughtry, the only Rengalla with tertiary powers (in her case, the ability of foresight) had managed to bring the Rengalla together, to harness her powers, and to defeat the leader of the Dalshie (*and* save Morgan's life, but that was a story for another day). But there still might be rogue Dalshie out there.

The Dalshie were former Rengalla who used dark magic, who'd succumbed to its allure, and because the Rengalla's powers had been out of balance until Daughtry discovered the key, they'd *all* been susceptible to losing control, to losing themselves, their friends, their family.

And they had.

They had all lost loved ones to the soulless monsters who thrived on the pain of others.

So, while the Dalshie, on the whole, were all but eliminated, the shield remained in place, their young and innocent kept inside it because they still had to be careful, because they couldn't trust in the fragile peace.

They'd let their guard down too many times in the past.

Until they were certain that every single Dalshie had been wiped off the planet, the LexTal, the senior, intermediate, and junior soldiers wouldn't fully relax.

And hell, they probably wouldn't relax even then.

Because they still lived in the remote mountainous region of Tennessee, and case in point, their healer, Suz, had been attacked by a fucking *bear* not too long before. Not to mention there were the rattlesnakes, the copperheads, the brown recluse spiders, and the black widows.

Hell, they also had poison ivy, ticks, and fucking skunks. Less terrifying...or perhaps, *more* terrifying, just in a different way.

So, no, they wouldn't ever completely relax, not when they had innocents to take care of, to protect.

Because the last time a skunk got loose inside the Colony...

He shuddered; his nose still burned just from the memory of the stench.

But none of that explained why Darcy hadn't shown up for her shift.

Despite the chip on her shoulder that was the size of a fucking tank and the questions she needed to have answered that often seemed to number in the thousands, she was reliable. Never late. Never called off a shift on patrol, assignment, or working in the kitchens, the classrooms, or the armory. Darcy did her duty.

Always.

So, for her not to be here today...something was off.

And it was something more than because she'd worked late the night before. It was...

Off.

And that this had happened the morning after he'd passed on the envelope from Dante? Yeah, that didn't sit right with him.

As prickly as she was, she was vulnerable beneath.

But he also had a shift to cover, a hole to fill. He couldn't just disappear, couldn't go and track her down, not when he was the most senior soldier in charge of this set of patrols, not when he was supposed to be overseeing everything so Daughtry, Cody, and company could scout out a good perimeter for the shield.

He needed to be here.

And as much as everyone liked to tease him for being a loudmouth shit stirrer, he took his responsibilities seriously. He didn't fuck around with the people he loved—and that love extended right down to the newest lives.

Including the one Daughtry was now carrying out the front doors of the Colony.

Flanked by Cody and John, with Alex a step in front of her, she looked like a queen in a procession, her guards surrounding her. Which, to her chagrin, probably was the truth. Dee was powerful, more so than any other Rengalla, but...Morgan wasn't the only one with protective instincts.

Sweeping forward, he dodged around Alex—and the recently promoted soldier sighed but didn't comment or try and halt him (as most people had learned was the correct way to deal with his shenanigans. Because he wouldn't stop what he wanted to do, and because he was harmless, at least to those... say it with him...he loved).

And Cody and Dee's baby was his favoritest person who he loved.

A mop of red hair, bright green eyes, an infectious smile, and Colby was fucking adorable. Almost enough to make Morgan want one of his own—minus the poopy diapers, up at all hours of the night, the fussy, the—

Hell, who was he kidding?

He'd be down to make one of these creatures.

Scanning his surroundings was instinctual, something he always did, but with the tiny baby nearby, he did another scan. Then scooped up the baby and fell into step beside Cody and John.

"We've got a hole on the green route. I'm going to fill it"—he blew a raspberry on Colby's tummy—"will you be able to oversee?" he asked John. "Or should I call in Monroe?"

Cody frowned. "Who didn't show?"

He didn't like having to reveal, "Darcy."

Now John joined Cody in frowning. "That's not typical."

"She had a migraine," he blurted, covering for her when he really fucking shouldn't. He *knew* he shouldn't. But he also knew that he couldn't throw her under the bus, not when something was wrong, not when he knew that in the marrow of his bones. "Showed up," added, "but I sent her home to sleep it off."

That cleared the frowns, and John nodded. "I'll supervise. You'll pick up the green route."

Morgan blew one more raspberry before he handed Colby back to Dee. "I needed the steps anyway," he said, pursing his lips at Cody, blowing his fellow LexTal a kiss. "This body doesn't look this good unless I close my rings every single day."

Cody sighed, rolled his eyes, but didn't comment.

He tugged the tablet out from his pocket, tossed it to John, and then went off to patrol the green route.

Had to get those steps in.

CHAPTER THREE

Darcy

KNOCKING HAD her peeling back her lids, barely able to lift them.

Had someone attached concrete blocks to her lashes? Probably not.

Was it the bottle of rum she'd nearly drained? Maybe.

The contents of the letter? Definitely.

Which was why she'd torn it to pieces and then used her magic to turn it to ash.

The knocking intensified.

She managed to get those concrete blocks off her eyelids, got her brain working enough to recognize that the knocking was actually knocking at her door rather than knocking in her brain, along with pounding from her lovely hangover.

Groaning, she rolled to her other side, pulled the pillow over her head, and ignored the knocking.

Eventually, the noise cut off.

"Good," she muttered, holding the pillow tighter, drawing it over her ears, burrowing down into her covers, and desperate to go back to before she'd read the letter.

Even with her pillow earmuffs, even with the hangover and the pounding in her skull, she didn't miss the sound of her door opening. She bit back a curse.

Should have known that it wouldn't be that easy.

Maybe if she held *very* still, they would think she was asleep and just leave her with her misery, and then she could sleep for however long it took for her to pull her shields back around her and forget the contents of that *fucking* letter.

Footsteps in her hallway.

Near her bed.

Her light flicked on, and even through her pillow shield, she winced. Too much rum. Too. Much. *Rum.* The mattress dipped as whoever it was sank down next to her.

The question to whoever it was answered approximately one second later.

"I know you're awake," Morgan said.

She went stiff.

Which was something that no asleep person would do. Stupid, right? And Morgan knew it, too, either the stupid or awake part, or both, she supposed. Not that it mattered because she was very stupid and very awake and very much pulling the pillow from her face and ears and sitting up with a sigh.

"Is breaking and entering on the list of LexTal duties nowadays?" she grumbled.

A pause. Then, "It is when I have an intermediate soldier who doesn't show up for her shift."

Alertness slammed into her with all the force of a Mack Truck. "A—*what?*" She gasped, spun toward the nightstand, and snatched up her cell. It wasn't. It couldn't be—she *couldn't* have missed her shift. She was on from eight in the morning until one in the…

"Oh fuck," she breathed.

It was four.

Four fucking o'clock in the afternoon and—

In all her fuckups, she'd never missed a shift.

Never.

Even when she'd gotten passed up for advancement, even after she'd moved here and felt like she didn't fit in, even after her dad…

She closed her eyes, dropped her chin to her chest.

"I'll go to Cody, to Dante and Dee," she murmured. "Apologize. Explain"—how in the fuck she was going to explain that she'd missed her shift because her head was fucked up and she'd drunk herself into oblivion was beyond her—"apologize," she repeated, "and own up."

Morgan's face did a thing.

A soft thing. A *dangerous* thing. "It's fine," he began.

"It's *not* fine," she whispered. "I've never done that before. It's just—" She remembered who she was talking to and cut herself off. "I'll apologize and own up to my mistake."

Probably she'd be pulled off patrols, be made to do more kitchen and armory and bathroom, and God help her, she was probably going to have to do more shifts in the garden. It would be fine…just so long as she kept her powers to herself.

"It's *fine*," Morgan said again.

She opened her mouth to argue.

"I told Cody you had a migraine," he said, "and by the looks of your face and that empty bottle of rum on your nightstand, I'm guessing the headache you've got is a lot worse than one."

He lied for her.

What in the fuck all?

Rage slithered down her spine, filling her limbs with frost, shooting barbed spikes out of her fingertips that curled, ready to attack, lathering itself on her tongue, sharp retorts at the ready. "How dare—"

Morgan's mouth tipped up. "You can put that chip back on your shoulder in a minute. Right now, you're going to set it on the nightstand and tell me what was in the letter and why it caused you to drink yourself into a stupor."

How the fuck did he know?

How *the fuck* did he know?

Well, the how didn't matter so much as the fact that he *did* know. But she wasn't going to let him know that she knew that he *knew* and—

Fuck it all.

That was both too many *knews* and too few answers for why the hell he'd lied to cover up her fuckup.

Further that, she wasn't relinquishing her chip, thank her very much.

It was fucking Superglued to her shoulder and there it would stay for all the rest of her days. That was both the simple truth and the really fucking complicated one and—

Fingers brushing hers—no *fingers* taking her cell from her hand and tossing it on her nightstand. "What was in the letter, Pem?"

Unbidden, her eyes began to burn at the soft question— stupid fucking *emotions*.

Darcy kept her gaze on her hands, on the warm, golden skin covering Morgan's, the soft lines occasionally crisscrossing the space—probably when he'd decided to forgo a healer's magic, leaving Suz and her trainees' powers so they could be used on others. Because Morgan was good, and she was...

No.

A blink. Silent shoring of her spine, her heart, her insides.

For a minute (for a week), she'd thought she could be with him forever, thought he might be the one person—

More shoring.

Her chin came up.

Because *he* hadn't thought she could be that person for him, hadn't thought in terms of forever.

He'd thought in terms of days—of a week.

So no, he didn't get to barge into her life, pretending to be concerned, not when he hadn't been concerned while he'd been taking a meat pulverizer to her heart.

She rolled off the bed opposite him—not putting it past him

to try and snag her arm, to haul her against him and pin her with his body until she relented. Because she would *have* to relent. Because he was a better fighter and stronger and he *could* pin her, as much as that pained her to admit.

He stood, but she'd formulated a plan before she'd moved, which was why she was faster.

Namely that she was able to shove her feet into shoes, snag her hoodie, and get to the door before he moved.

But not *out* the door.

Instead, she ended up in the worst possible position— pinned between him and the door. And God, that was good. To have his strong, muscled front against her back, his scent— sunflowers and cayenne—surrounding her, filling up her pores, soaking into her skin, her nose, her tongue.

One week.

Nearly a decade before.

The best sex of her life.

And it might as well have occurred a *heartbeat* before, her pussy still throbbing, his cum still leaking out to coat the tops of her thighs, her breathing still elevated, her skin covered in a sheen of sweat. Because him being this close—when she'd been so careful to keep her distance, taking assignments at other Rengallan strongholds, taking another one keeping a low-key eye on Daughtry before she'd been pulled from any "danger- ous, undercover work" because she was a fucking loose cannon who couldn't be trusted with anything more than plants and hanging targets and changing lightbulbs—had longing tearing through her, need and desire twining through her middle, sliding up between her legs, pulsing across her breasts, dipping down into her liquid heat.

This man made her want to…

This man made her *want*…

No.

"Come on, Pem," he cajoled, one of his hands dropping to her waist, the other next to her head, caging her in, making all that want flare with even more urgency. But...she frowned, tried to grasp on to the sensation, because it almost seemed as though it wasn't coming solely from her—

"Pem," he said again, less cajoling and more filled with an order.

She blinked, the sensation disappeared, and she came back into herself. Because this man might be able to give her orders outside this room when it came to the protection of their people.

But in here, he didn't get a say.

Except...you really liked it when he did have a say in this room. In his rooms. In the shower and the broom closet and the gardens and—

She straightened her shoulders. "Why do you keep calling me that?"

"What was in the note?"

Another flare—this time of annoyance, which thankfully tempered the last of the need, gave her the clarity of mind to buck against him and spin in his hold, to face him head-on and—

Oh.

That was nice.

The press of his front to hers.

All that hard of him against all of her. The cage tightening, his head dipping, his nose dragging along her throat as he exhaled, the heat of his breath making goose bumps prickle on her arms, desire slide down her spine.

But she was steel.

Or pretending to be anyway.

So, she lifted her chin, narrowed her eyes, held tight to the flicker of annoyance, and deliberately walled away the desire, even when his voice rumbled as he dropped his head again, inhaled against her skin, "Jasmine," he murmured. "You smell like jasmine."

She liked that.

Liked the rasp and the touch and him being so close and—

No. No, she didn't. She hated it, *despised* it, despised *him*.

"What was in the note, baby?" Still soft, still touching her. Still...trying to manipulate her to get something that he wanted.

No matter the cost.

The *cost.*

That slid over her in a cold wave, dousing those embers of desire, extinguishing the fury, as pain—*so much* fucking pain— took over.

Morgan's head jerked up, surprise flaring in his hazel eyes, "Darcy, what's—"

But he'd given her the opening she needed.

A sharp kick to his shin surprised him, knocked him back a pace. Another to his groin had him groaning and bending at the waist, even as he still reached for her.

She spun, guilt tearing through her—but what else was new?—raised her elbow and—

Crack!

Caught him in the cheek, just below the eye.

"Fuck," he cursed, and the bastard still reached for her, ignoring the onslaught, hands outstretched, and she knew —*knew*—she'd bought herself all the time she could for her escape.

Morgan wouldn't fight back, wouldn't want to hurt her (more guilt...because she'd hurt him).

But he *would* restrain her, and he would press and press and *press* until she told him.

And...

She couldn't go there. Not yet. Not now.

Maybe not ever.

So, when he reached for her again, she swung. Hard and fast, a quick jab that collided with his nose with a sickening *crunch.* Blood began pouring out, blood that he ignored, blood that covered her hand when she punched him again. Blood that got into her mouth, a coppery tang that coated her tongue.

"Stop," he growled, reaching for her.

She threw another punch. It connected. Again.

But this one was only a glancing blow because he dodged, just not enough to avoid her fist.

He jumped back and glared at her, still slightly hunched from the groin kick, his nose actively bleeding, his eye and cheekbone already blackening.

And Darcy did the only thing she could—

Fumbled for the knob behind her, whipped open and slammed the door shut after she dove through, and then...she used her fire magic to seal the metal door to the metal frame, melting the two together in an instant.

And then...she ran.

CHAPTER FOUR

Morgan

HE CURSED a blue streak when he grabbed the doorknob, intending to go after Darcy, and burned the fuck out of his hand.

Glancing at it, he saw the metal was glowing, knew that the only reason he didn't end up with third-degree burns was because his skin was covered in a thin shield to protect from a magical attack.

This wasn't an attack—or at least not the doorknob part, anyway.

The rest...hell, that wasn't an attack, either. Not really. Instead, it was a cornered animal, terrified and fighting to be free, one he had continued to provoke when he should have stopped and considered.

Why *hadn't* he stopped?

Yeah, he was a shit stirrer. Yeah, he liked to push people's buttons. But not like that. Not pressing a scared woman until she lashed out. *Fuck*. Normally, he would have taken a breath, used his training. He had fucking decades of it.

But, in that moment, it was as though his mind had gone foggy, as if all his thoughts were twisted together, spinning and whirling, emotions flying through him like meteors—desire, frustration, need, annoyance, pleasure, fear—

Fear?

He frowned. Shook it off.

No, it couldn't have been fear.

He was clearly off his game. Hence, the groin shot and the bloody nose, and the—he reached up, touched his eye—what was certainly going to be a shiner.

Yeah, he hadn't been fighting back, but Darcy had surprised him with the initial moves, made it difficult to block her as she kept him guessing. "Well, fuck," he muttered, pushing it out of his mind. He'd deal with it later. For now, he needed to get out of this room.

Pale brown flames still flickered along the metal, and he took a breath, summoned some water (to douse) and air (to choke) the magic, and put out the flames. Gold and brown and green sparks that matched the color of his eyes burst to life on his palms and then gathered into thin tendrils, and then into larger strands. It took mere seconds before they were cascading toward the door, twining with the pale brown of Darcy's remnants of magic, battling those dredges as he put out the flames. He started at that first touch, a strange sensation rippling through him, something both right and wrong at the same time, but it was there and gone so quickly that he struggled to pinpoint exactly what had happened.

Probably because his balls hurt like motherfuckers and his nose was dripping blood all over Darcy's floor.

Finally, the flames were out, so he cut his magic and examined the door.

It was warped along the edges, the frame and panel molded together, locking him in, putting a firm barricade between himself and Darcy, and despite the aching balls, the throbbing cheek, Morgan couldn't help but grin.

So fucking fierce.

He shook out his stinging palm, glanced at the door one more time, and then sent some more magic its way. He'd need to cool down the metal before he could get out of there, make sure it wasn't going to start a fire. Though, he supposed it wouldn't, not when—even in her obvious panic—Darcy had been careful to only burn the metal and none of the surrounding material of the wall.

But...he wasn't going to pass up this opportunity to snoop, even *if* he could just teleport out, not when she was being so cagey about the letter.

What had Dante passed on that had her so messed up?

He didn't know, but as he turned and surveyed the contents of her quarters, Morgan knew he was damned sure going to find out.

———

BUT...HE *didn't* find out.

Even though he'd snooped through every drawer and cupboard. Even though he'd checked under the bed and beneath the mattress. Even long after he felt guilty for invading her privacy (but that guilt didn't stop him from rustling through the drawers in her bathroom vanity), he continued searching.

And came to three conclusions.

One, Darcy had destroyed the letter (this conclusion was developed upon the discovery of ashes in her trash can— because yes, he'd even looked in the trash can).

Two, Darcy had very few personal effects.

Three, he should have noticed that before, when he was fucking her in this very room. But...they'd spent more time in his rooms, and hell, their short-lived time together was...well, *short-lived.*

None of that changed the fact that she had very little.

No pictures. No scrapbooks. No teddy bears from her childhood. Her drawers and closets were filled with strictly functional items.

T-shirts in one.

Jeans in another.

A drawer for knives. One for guns and another for ammo. There were books (dry tomes on military tactics, geography, and history) on her desk, along with a laptop with a locked screen (and a password he couldn't open or guess because...he'd tried). Her closet held exactly two dresses—a simple black one he'd seen her wear to parties at the Colony, and a sage green one she'd worn to Daughtry and Cody's wedding—and four pairs of shoes. Two of those were combat boots. One was a pair of sneakers. And the last were slender black heels.

Her bathroom wasn't much better.

Cheap shampoo and conditioner. A bar of soap. A toothbrush, toothpaste, and lip balm.

He did unearth a small makeup kit buried behind some towels and a couple of old boxes of hair color. Darcy used to dye her hair a deep black with pops of color near her face, but he hadn't seen her do that in...

He frowned.

Years now, he supposed.

Maybe since she and Daughtry had returned to the Colony.

Her hair had faded until she'd eventually returned to her natural dirty blonde color.

Sighing as he put the dye back into the linen closet, Morgan left the bathroom and surveyed Darcy's quarters. He had the insane urge to buy a fucking candle for the place—jasmine to smell like her, or maybe something fruity. And he could hang a picture up on the wall, something to brighten the space and—

He chuckled darkly. She'd sooner tear it down, just because he'd dared to put one up, and probably would whack him upside the head with it. *Then* chuck it in the trash.

But…he didn't like the idea of her living in all this dreary, this plain, this dark and dim and look, it wasn't like the Rengalla skimped on the finishes. Her rooms were nice (minus the scorched door), with wood floors and oil-rubbed bronze fixtures and knobs, built-in cabinets.

His mom was a designer, and she'd made sure that each space was decorated in a way that was homey and warm.

Darcy, however, had managed to undo that.

Maybe it was the white walls (usually painted by the people living in the space because his mom liked to give everyone options). Maybe it was the lack of personal effects and decor. Aside from a single lamp on her nightstand and one on her desk, there was not one extra item that didn't have function.

Then add in that three of the six bulbs were out in the recessed lights overhead, the faded and thin bedcovers, the single flat pillow…and Darcy had made the space sad.

So yeah, he wanted to buy a candle or a painting or a throw pillow. He *wanted* to turn his mom loose on the space.

But…

Wasn't going to happen. The second for sure. It wasn't his place to intervene here. He'd had a fling with her years before. They were barely acquaintances now, co-workers and nothing more. He teleported out (because, thankfully, while the shield blocked teleporting in out and out of The Colony's shield, he could teleport within the actual buildings), and returned to his own quarters, cleaned the blood off his face, glamoured his nose and bruised eye (because seriously, he did *not* want to explain what happened to anyone, least of all to his brothers). Then, after he'd changed his clothes, he made a call into maintenance to get Darcy a new door.

But after he hung up, he found that he couldn't put his cell back in his pocket.

Instead, his fingers danced across the screen, opening an app, putting a few things in his online cart. Hitting "Order" and then hitting the garage, checking out a vehicle, and driving down the mountain into town.

To pick up that order.

And it might have included a candle...or five.

And fuck it, he tossed in a throw pillow for good measure.

CHAPTER FIVE

Darcy

SHE SHOULDN'T BE HERE.

It wasn't a place of happy memories.

It was a keeper of doom—and she meant that without any ironic dramatic tendencies. This wasn't a dramady.

It was her life.

Sighing, she got out of her car and strode up the walkway to the front door.

A thread of her magic slid forward without thought, guiding itself into a lock that she probably should have figured would be closed to her, her magic blocked out after she'd left against his wishes. But even as she processed that the door would no doubt be locked to her, there was a shuddering in the shield surrounding the door, and the magic unfurled.

She reached for the knob and turned it, sighing when it was unlocked, when it swung open.

Some of the older Rengalla—her father included—relied too much on magic.

But magic failed, magic eroded, magic...sometimes couldn't do enough.

To protect. To heal. To—

She stepped inside, wincing at the stale smell in the air. Fried food and rotten milk. Mildew and dust and…old.

It smelled *old*.

"Fuck," she whispered, striding through the house and into the kitchen. The lights worked, which was a miracle—though not so much, she supposed, when she considered that it was probably residual magic fueling them rather than the human power grid.

Not enough to fuel the fridge, though.

Which she discovered when she opened the door. All the food inside had gone foul, the mold inside having seemingly grown mold. The smell…well, the smell was something indescribable. It burned, literally *burned* her nostrils, made her eyes water, made her gag so violently that she slammed the refrigerator shut and ran out the front door, sitting down on the half-rotted steps and breathing slowly in and out through her mouth.

God, that smell, she could still taste it on her tongue, feel it soaking into her pores.

Why was she here?

She should just leave. Just close the door, lock it, and get the fuck out of here and never come back. Hell, she didn't even have to lock the door. She could leave it open, let the critters take roost (if they could stand the smell). Or maybe it was better to light the entire thing on fire, to let it burn to ashes, to erase the memories of what took place here.

But…

She couldn't.

Not when there was the spot in the kitchen where her mom had measured her, tiny scratches in the old logs, so faint after all these years that they were barely visible.

Not when there was probably the small cookie jar still hidden at the back of the cabinet's top shelf above the fridge.

The cookie jar her mom had made in her pottery studio, the pale blue glaze Darcy's personal favorite. God, growing up she'd had so many of those small clay and ceramic trinkets lined up on shelves in her room, positioned in the windows.

Sometimes when she looked up at the sky, she still saw that particular shade of pale blue laced with wisps of white.

Her mom up there.

Her mom—

Gone because there was no *up there* and she had been on this planet long enough to know that, had seen too many things, had known too many monsters to believe otherwise.

But she couldn't shake the feeling, the niggle, the *hope* that maybe her mom occasionally glimpsed between the clouds, looked down on Darcy, and was…proud.

A sigh, the sound *pfting* out from between her lips.

Thinking.

She was doing too much of it.

Because she hadn't done much in her life to be proud of, and…because her mom was gone, those pale blue trinkets reduced to shards, shattered on the floor, and left for her to clean up.

Sweeping the broken pieces. Prepping the body.

Making the calls.

Avoiding the yelling, the fists, the—

"Enough."

She pushed to her feet, and though her magic flickered at her fingertips, roiled just beneath the surface of her skin, her fire at the ready, the temptation to turn it all to ash *right there*, Darcy extinguished her powers, sucked in another breath, released it slowly, and then, inhaling and exhaling through her nose, she went back into the house.

Went to the kitchen.

Climbed up onto the countertop next to the fridge.

Opened the cabinet door.

Reached for the back corner of the top shelf.
Her fingers encountered nothing but dust...
And a single shard of glazed clay.

CHAPTER SIX

Morgan

THE NEW DOOR to Darcy's quarters had been installed.

The paint had been touched-up both inside and out, erasing any trace of what had happened.

He'd placed a candle on her desk, three more stored in her linen closet for (hopefully) future use, and a romantic comedy book had made its way onto her bookshelf. Her bed had new soft sheets, two throw pillows, and a blanket he'd put into his cart at the big box store that had been quickly accompanied by a new set of bedding.

And on the wall, he'd hung a painting, done in shades of pale blue and white, swirled together in a way that almost resembled a partly cloudy sky.

Morgan had been heading out of the home goods section, intent on the registers when the image of that blue and white had popped into his brain, nearly taking over his senses, and then he'd turned, seen the canvas, and…it had joined the party in his cart.

Now it was on Darcy's wall.

She was going to be pissed at both his snooping and his

presumption, but hopefully the drawer full of chocolate in her nightstand would buy him some grace.

He paused, considered that, knew it wouldn't buy him any grace in the least.

But…he'd take her sass and her fire. So long as it erased the cold, pained look that had been in her eyes.

He straightened the blanket on the bed—the one he'd snuck in here well after the maintenance team had replaced her door—not wanting to be pumped for information, not wanting them to make the connection between him and Darcy and whatever was going on between them.

Nothing.

There was *nothing* going on between them.

Except, he didn't buy that lie, not even in his own mind. Because he'd broken them off before they had barely begun years ago, knowing that he didn't have time for a relationship when he'd been promoted to a LexTal—the highest order of soldiers amongst the Rengalla. But more than that, he'd broken things off because things would have been too complicated. He couldn't be in a relationship with a subordinate, not freshly into a leadership position.

And Darcy had just been beginning her soldier training.

It wouldn't have been fair to her.

She needed space to become her own person, her own soldier. Especially when she'd been new to the Colony, just establishing her place there.

She didn't need him to take over.

So, they'd had their fun, and then he'd ended things before it became more.

But he'd handled it poorly, and she hadn't forgiven him, and hell, he'd grasped on to any opportunity to be pissed at her, to revel in her faults. Because that was easier, easier to pretend he couldn't stand her, especially when the temptation to go back and beg her to forgive him, to weasel his way into her bed was intense.

And more difficult to ignore every time he saw her.

So, he hadn't.

Hadn't seen her.

Now…he *had*. And it was bigger, more intense than ever. A deep itch or niggling or maybe, just a painful throbbing that told him he'd seriously fucked up by cutting things off between them, that he'd missed something, missed out on *her*.

Which was why he was standing in her room, fussing with the placement of that blanket, waiting for her to come back.

As he'd been doing for hours.

So much so that it was past midnight and he had to be up in five hours for a shift, and it was going to be hell to drag himself out of bed because he really liked his mattress, and really fucking hated being off of it before the sun came up.

But he also didn't want to leave before he'd laid eyes on Darcy.

Sighing, he settled on the edge of her bed, pulled out his phone, and started playing the game he was addicted to, serving hungry diners tiny plates of hamburgers and bowls of soup, trying to get his chain bonus, his color match, and not lose any hearts.

Pretty soon, though, his day caught up to him, and he found his eyes growing heavy.

Just a second.

Just for *one* sec…

———

THE CLICK HAD sudden awareness flooding Morgan's body, but his training had him staying in position, holding still, keeping his breathing steady, and listening to the door open and close.

Not trying to be quiet.

Not attempting to sneak up—

No. *He* was the interloper, he realized, the rest of his brain coming online. This was Darcy's room. Darcy's bed.

And Darcy was coming home.

Fuck.

Unless…someone was coming to meet her, to wait in her bed, to *claim* her.

For one second, rage tore through him, visceral and intense and so out of nowhere that his breathing stalled as that feeling of possession rippled through him. The urge to make her his was so fierce that he nearly launched himself out of the bed to tackle the bastard who'd thought to come into her rooms.

She was his.

His.

Then her scent hit his nose.

Jasmine, crawling up a trellis, winding its way through his senses, and that moment of temporary insanity faded, reason returning.

He resumed his breathing, keeping it slow and steady, even when he heard her footsteps halt suddenly, when he heard the sharp intake of breath, when he heard them pick up again as she approached the bed and halted.

A shadow crossing his closed eyelids.

A change in the air surrounding him.

A…

She poked him. *Hard.* And it took everything in him to not flinch, to not react, to not snag her wrist and yank her down, to pin her beneath him and the mattress, to—

"Morgan!" she hissed.

He kept his breathing steady, didn't so much as flicker an eyelid, even as she groaned—and not quietly, either.

Another poke. Another use of his name as a curse.

Another hiss of breath.

Another—

Sigh.

Her footsteps moving away…toward her desk. He slit his

eyes, saw her studying the candle like it was a rattlesnake about to strike. Then quickly closed them when she spun around, probably studying the linens, the new pillows, the throw, the painting now taking up a large portion of the formerly naked wall.

This time her sigh was pained.

No…her sigh sounded normal. It was something else that was pained…something in his mind…something that was coming from…*her* mind.

He went still.

Absolutely still, every muscle in his body going rigid, but by some miracle, Darcy didn't notice that he'd betrayed himself.

And he knew—he *knew*—it was because she was in turmoil over the candle.

Complete turmoil, her mind a writhing mass of emotions—old and new, pained and not. "Raspberries," she whispered into the quiet of the room. "Fucking rasp—" Her voice broke, moisture in her words, and he knew that if he could sit up and look into her eyes without betraying himself, without betraying the fucking nuclear bomb he'd just discovered, he would have seen them filled with tears.

And fuck betraying what he'd discovered, fuck betraying the idiotic farce that he'd been holding on to. Darcy was hurting and near tears, and he'd never seen her cry—

No.

He'd seen her cry *once*.

When he'd ended things with her.

She'd nodded and said that she understood, but when she'd turned to walk away, he'd seen the tears in her eyes, the glittering drop sliding down her cheek.

Now she was a millimeter away from crying over a candle and he knew…he *knew* that he couldn't let that happen.

He started to sit up, but the footsteps beat him to action.

They flew down the hallway toward Darcy's front door, and he'd barely had his feet on the floor before the door slammed shut. He moved, following her, so off his game by what he'd discovered moments before that he actually forgot he could teleport.

Which meant he used human speed as he moved out of Darcy's bedroom, down her hallway, through her new front door, and out, head swiveling as he looked for her.

Which *meant*, there wasn't a trace of her, not a sound or a thread of magic, even though the walls usually siphoned off their extra magic, drawing it into the Colony, using it to fuel the lights, power the air conditioning and furnace, the computers and smoke detectors.

The Rengalla were their own power plants.

But there wasn't a trace of the pale brown on the walls, nor any jasmine in the air.

She'd shielded herself...and disappeared.

He wasn't surprised. Because even though she was only an intermediate soldier, even though she hadn't been promoted several times, those times she'd been passed over hadn't been because she wasn't talented.

Darcy was skilled.

Very much so.

It was just her attitude that sucked.

But there wasn't so much as a flicker of that attitude.

Morgan thrust a hand through his hair, stifled his curse. She couldn't be far. She—

He felt *it*.

Felt her, felt...

Their bond.

It was there, a slender thread of connection that he could feel, just barely sense in the back of his mind, a tendril of her magic twined with his, brown tangled with hazel, his powers woven with hers. Something foreign and yet, something completely natural.

And...something that was slightly stronger when he turned to the right.

CHAPTER SEVEN

Darcy

SHE HAD COMPLETELY LOST IT.

Over a fucking raspberry-scented candle.

Because…

The memories were strong, had been exposed, what was normally encased in concrete and steel and shoved deep fucking down was open to the air, a throbbing wound.

And then she'd walked into her quarters and smelled him.

She'd thought it was because of their altercation earlier. Fuck. She'd been so off her game that she hadn't even processed that she shouldn't have been able to walk right in, that the panel hadn't even been locked, that the door she'd all but destroyed hours earlier had been replaced and functioned like…well, like an actual door.

She shouldn't have been able to get into her rooms.

Not without melting her way in.

Hell, she'd been planning on sleeping in one of the empty rooms surrounding her quarters—empty since she lived in the older section of the Colony. But…the broken cookie jar, the wooden panel with small scratches that documented her height, her old room with the shelves, empty of anything except memories.

And a house in disrepair, broken and foul-smelling and full of evidence of a sad, old man.

A sad, old man who'd...

She shook her head.

Who'd given words that sliced. Who'd torn down happy memories, a happy place. And who'd...before she'd left, had beaten her until she was bloody, until she'd barely been able to move, until she'd looked in the mirror and hadn't recognized herself.

Broken.

Burned by flames.

Reduced to ashes.

Smoking, smoldering, floating away on the air, mere wisps blown in all directions. Gone forever.

She'd tried desperately to grasp hold of those filaments, to gather them up, to hold them close and return them to their proper location, but it had proved to be an impossible task. Darcy had been changed. Forever.

And that was about the time she'd decided fuck all with living her life for anyone else.

She was going to do what she wanted, when she wanted, and if someone else had an issue with that, then they could just fuck right off. Unfortunately, that wasn't exactly conducive with a chain of command. Not that she'd given a damn. She wanted to learn how to protect herself. She wanted to learn how to kill Dalshie.

Mission accomplished.

Which was why she was hiding in a fucking broom closet.

Right.

Scared of a man who'd been sleeping in her bed, who'd bought her a candle and a painting and new fucking linens.

Who'd woken up and tried to follow her. Who'd probably demand an explanation for her running (times two), or who'd...

hell, who was she kidding? He'd probably kick her ass for her little stunt earlier.

Fuck.

She'd melted a door to its frame.

She could have lit the Colony on fire, set off the alarms, triggered an evacuation (and yes, she was ignoring the fact that her home base was full of magical people, most of whom—even the children—had basic control over their elemental powers, including fire, so the likelihood of her actually burning down the place was slim...to none). The point was that—as usual—she had thought of herself and not her actions, and she'd put people at risk.

And now she was hiding in a broom closet, surrounded by her good friends, Clorox and Windex.

Because even though the Rengalla had powers, could suck up dust and shine chandeliers, those kinds of tasks tended to be a waste of their magic.

Everyone had a limited amount of power, and imagine what their chagrin might be if they didn't have enough left to do what they needed because they'd decided to wipe off some baseboards.

Or slaughter some Dalshie.

Cute.

Cleaning baseboards and decapitation. Totally natural companions.

Sighing, she slid down along the wall, sinking to her bottom, resting her elbows on her knees.

She'd just wait here, wait until the coast was clear, wait until she could hide from the shitshow she'd made of her fucking life. Hide from the memories. Hide from—

The door swung open.

Light blinded her, and she blinked, trying to see who'd opened the door...even though she already knew.

Morgan.

Of course, it was Morgan.

Some part of her knew he'd find her. Some part of her...had sensed him getting closer.

Darcy frowned. What? No. That wasn't right. That couldn't be right. That—

He leaned against the frame, crossed his arms over his chest. "I know what you're thinking," he said calmly. As though she hadn't fucking made him bleed earlier in the day. As though he hadn't fixed her door and filled her quarters with a raspberry candle and new linens and a painting that reminded her of her mom.

And that candle...

Damn, why had he picked that?

Why—

Fuck. The *why* didn't matter.

She should have welded *this* door shut. Then she and her friends, Windex and Clorox, could just live in here forever, bonding over dust bunnies in the corners and shelves she was too short to reach the top of.

She could be fresh-smelling and really clean.

But...she might not live very long if the only things she had to drink were cleaning products.

"You're thinking you should have welded this door shut."

She blinked.

"And, for some reason, about drinking cleaning products."

She blinked again.

"Do you know why that is?"

A sick sort of horror was twining through her, coiling together, crawling up the back of her throat. Because she could feel him, too. She could *hear* him. She could—

No. No, this wasn't right. This couldn't be right. This couldn't—

Fingers grasping her chin, tilting her head so she was ensnared in an intense hazel gaze. "It's right," he said simply.

No. No. Not right. Not—

"It's *right*."

Darcy wasn't listening to him, not when she was too busy studying what was happening in her brain, what was happening with her powers.

Because they weren't her powers, or not *solely* hers, not any longer.

Her boring brown was now intertwined with hazel, with green and gold and a pretty russet color. All twisted together, braided in a way she knew meant they wouldn't ever truly be separated. Already, they were too mixed up, too knotted, too tangled—

Wait.

Daughtry and Cody's bond almost broke.

When they'd been newly together, when they'd been the first Rengallan couple to bond in centuries, Dee having unlocked (without knowing it) the key to their faltering magic, the infectious dark powers creating Dalshie, they'd separated…

And the bond had almost fractured.

There had to be a way to stop *this* one.

It was just barely formed, just a baby. It would be easy to shatter. It *had* to be.

Those fingers on her chin tightened, those gorgeous hazel eyes blazed, the link in her mind pulsed as fury slid from his mind to hers.

And then she heard the words.

In her ears…and in her brain.

"No," he said. "No, you fucking won't."

Break the bond.

Give up their magic.

Because that was the only way to break the bond. They separated. They purposefully let their connection grow weak, didn't nurture it with love and affection, the bond would fray. It would shatter. It would break…and they both would lose their magic.

It was the bond's way of tying them together, linking two

people who'd make powerful offspring, DNA more important than love.

That wasn't fair.

But it was easier to think about it that way than to think of the love Cody and Dee, John and Alex, Mason and Gabby, Graham and Suz shared. The devotion the couples had toward each other, the way they made each other so fucking, deliriously happy.

Fuck. *Fuck.*

Darcy closed her eyes, unable to continue holding Morgan's gaze.

She couldn't. She. *Couldn't.*

She couldn't be tied to someone this way. She couldn't be tied to Morgan, the man who'd fucking broken her. She couldn't be tied to anyone.

God, if she had remembered anything important that day, it was the fucking disaster that came from thinking there were happy endings. They just didn't happen...at least not for her.

Not. For. Her.

That was the God's honest truth.

"What are you thinking?" Morgan asked.

She tugged her chin from his grip, stood. "Why don't *you* tell *me?*"

His lips twitched as he stood, as he leaned back against the doorframe and crossed his arms again. "I can't."

She lifted a brow.

He tapped his temple. "I'm having a problem with transmission at the moment."

"Good." She started to brush by him, but he caught her arm.

"I'm not letting you go, Pem."

"That's not your choice, *Morg.*"

And then she yanked out of his grip, strode down the hall. Passed her quarters, out the front door, ignoring Mac, who was on night sentry, and who'd seen her come in not too long before.

"Darcy, you o—"

She let the door slam shut behind her.

Then she walked through the shield, out into the cold darkness of the night, and…

Didn't stop.

Not to think. Not to worry. Not to remember.

She just walked.

CHAPTER EIGHT

Morgan

HE'D LET HER GO.

And now he thought that might have been a mistake.

No. It *had* been a mistake.

He'd gotten to his quarters, intending to give her some time to cool down, to approach her when the truth wasn't such a shock, wasn't so new.

But then he'd slapped his palm on the lock, started to push inside, and he'd known—*known*—that letting her walk off was a mistake.

He should be with her, shouldn't be leaving her alone.

Not when she was upset, and he didn't know why.

He stopped, closed his door, and retraced his steps.

Spotted a trail of her magic being absorbed into the wall, of *their* combined powers, and followed the wake to see where she'd gone, followed it all the way to the front exit of the Colony. But there were no wakes to be tracked outside, and Mac had said she hadn't so much as acknowledged him, let alone told him where she was going.

Just that she'd walked out. Straight out into the dark.

It was late.

The moon wasn't out, clouds filled the sky. Fuck, there weren't even stars to navigate by.

And she was out there, his *mate* was out there.

Concern and anger and fear rippled through him. Darcy was his to look out for, his to protect, his…just…*his*.

She might not know that yet, might not be ready to accept it.

But the bond didn't lie.

There was something between them, something that had been there even before the bond formed, something that had brought him to the big box store to buy a candle and bedding and the painting. Even before the last couple of days, his worry stoked by the note, their time together had been…intense.

Probably because although the bond couldn't have formed, not then, not before Daughtry had fixed everything, some sort of connection had still been there.

One that made it very difficult to back away, to let her go, even though he'd known that he needed to.

Twice now he'd done that.

Backed off when he should have stayed.

Now Darcy was out of the safety of the Colony. And she was upset, completely shaken to her core, freaked out about the bond. She might not be aware of her surroundings. Fuck, even though things had calmed down, it wasn't totally safe. She could encounter a Dalshie and not be prepared—*God*, it would be so easy for her life to be snuffed out by that dark magic, for her to be seriously hurt, especially when *he* wasn't there to make sure she was safe. Hell, even Dalshie aside, she might stumble across a bear, or a cougar, or a fucking rabid raccoon. Any of those could—

"Did she check out a car?" he asked Mac, who had trailed him out the door.

Mac glanced at the tablet he held, tapped a few times on the screen. "No." A beat. "Should I call someone?"

"No," Morgan said. "I'll go."

And then he didn't give Mac a chance to argue. He just walked across the grass, its dampness gathering on the toes of his boots, and moved toward the perimeter of the shield. The knitted strands of magic were translucent and softly glowing in the dark, disappearing beneath the surface of the ground. Deep enough so that enemies couldn't burrow in, but not so much as to be an unnecessary use of energy.

A breath.

Releasing his magic, allowing the gold and green and russet strands—now joined by the pale brown of Darcy's—slid forward and crawled up the shield, weaving in with the technicolor threads, gathering them together, tugging them gently to create an opening just wide enough for him to slip through.

As a soldier, his magic was keyed into the shield, as was Darcy's, so they didn't have to fight with the barrier or make a call to Daughtry to be let out in case of an emergency.

Some of the civilians were also coded, but none of the children.

For obvious reasons.

It was also coded against dark magic (also for obvious reasons), ensuring the Dalshie couldn't penetrate the barrier.

Morgan released his power, watched to make sure the hole closed behind him, and then he paused, closed his eyes, and focused on the link in his mind. Darcy was far enough away already that the bond was only a slender thread in the back of his brain, almost slippery and difficult to hold on to. But when he persisted, when he sent a tendril of his powers into it, when he narrowed in on that small connection, he could use it like he'd used it in the halls.

Like a radio transmitter—shifting one way and it faded, turning the other and it grew.

Following the direction of that slight bump in intensity, Morgan made his way through the trees, picking silently through the underbrush. There were lots of trails out in the forest, but none of them were easy to find at this time of night, not with his vision still adjusting to the dark, not without a flashlight.

Instead, he had to rely on his senses.

He became very aware of his feet and where he placed them, listening for any sounds of creatures or enemies...or for a certain Rengallan female who he was going to chase down and then give a piece of his mind.

But even still, he almost missed it.

The faint sound of breathing. The barest crinkle of a leaf.

There.

Straight ahead, just about twenty feet ahead, his eyes had adjusted enough that he could see Darcy silhouetted amongst the trees. She was sitting on a rock in between two trees, her back to him, her head tilted back, looking up at...the sky? No. It wasn't clear enough to see anything more than branches and darkness overhead.

"I know you're there," she said.

Quietly.

But the forest was so hushed that it easily reached his ears... or maybe...he frowned, concentrated on the bond. Maybe the words had been spoken directly into his mind.

It wasn't like he hadn't communicated telepathically before.

Tyler was his friend and a skilled telepath. Morgan had communicated that way plenty of times before. Hell, most missions they tried to communicate that way. It was certainly a lot more convenient than radios.

But it never felt like this.

"Darcy?" he thought.

She jerked, and he knew the feeling, even having experience with telepathy, *this* was different. More intimate somehow. As though her voice had stroked against the inside of his brain.

Silence.

Then she stood, her arms hanging at her sides, hands clenched into fists.

"You shouldn't be here," she said.

Deliberately *not* along the bond.

Because as Daughtry and Cody had first learned, communicating along the bond, spending time together, would strengthen the connection, would make it much less likely for it to break.

And Darcy didn't want the bond.

That hurt.

It shouldn't, not when he'd broken up with her, not when he'd hurt her years before. He'd chosen his job over their relationship, made it clear that she wasn't the top priority for him. Bondmates didn't do that. And now, years later, he still wanted her, wished he'd never broken up with her, and he was...fucked.

Because the bond was going to keep pulling them together—even if she fought it.

Because he wasn't going to have the time to win her over patiently. She was hurt and had *been* hurt by him, and it was going to be really hard to earn her trust.

The bond didn't help him in this case.

"Pem," he said, moving over to her, not touching her even though the bond screamed at him to take her in his arms, to hold her close, to kiss and stroke her until she forgot about the past and was willing to just look to the future.

She didn't respond, didn't look at him.

And he knew that he had to stop worrying about the past and why she was upset, had to stop wondering why she'd run because of a raspberry candle. He needed to focus on now, on winning her over, on keeping her safe.

On...convincing her to like him enough to want to keep the bond.

One, he didn't want to lose his magic.

Two, he didn't want to lose *her*.

Or maybe that should be the number one.

No, he knew, staring at Darcy, her features so delicate in the dim light. His heart clenched tight at the sight of the tension on her face, her tight jaw, he knew she *was* number one.

CHAPTER NINE

Darcy

H E WAS STANDING THERE STARING at her, and she was doing her best to not squirm under his study.

Because she didn't want the bond.

She *didn't*.

But...him standing so close, his focus solely on her, his scent in her nose, his heat warming her bare arm, stopping the cool of the night from sinking into her skin, and she couldn't deny that she liked it. Liked him near.

Liked...him.

No.

That was the bond. It was attempting to initiate her into the magical bond club. Have lots of hot, steamy sex and pop out some magically talented babies. It wasn't based on any real feelings, anything of substance.

So yeah, Darcy wanted to protect her people, to live her life as she wanted it. She wanted to keep her magic, and hell, the near-immortality thing wasn't all that bad either. But she didn't need a fucking control freak of a man who'd try to corner her and push her into telling him things she didn't want to. She didn't need—

A flicker of movement behind Morgan's shoulder.

"Down!" she yelled, reaching for his wrist and yanking him hard. He stumbled into her, his arms coming around her, but she sidestepped, dislodging his hold, and placed herself between him and the shadow in the distance, the threat to them both. Her magic flickered as it curled around her fingertips.

"What is it?" he asked, trying to step around her.

She thrust out an arm, used her magic to form a barrier in front of them, dutifully ignoring the fact that it was Bond Magic, and as thus, didn't look like *her* magic. Instead, it was a combination of hers and Morgan's.

But she didn't have time to worry over that.

Not when the branches of the undergrowth rustled, footsteps coming toward them.

A bear? A rogue Dalshie?

All she knew was that it was big and coming toward them.

Morgan didn't ask further questions, being a good enough soldier to deduce the concern based on the rustling and the direction of her gaze. He did, however, drop a hand on her shoulder and ready his magic.

It swirled around Darcy, and she knew with a single thought, he could have them miles away.

"Move behind me," he murmured, trying to tug her back.

She huffed out a laugh. "Don't pretend to care," she muttered.

His gaze found hers. "*What?*" he exclaimed, far too loud considering the rustling had intensified, and Darcy had coaxed them both back a step. Morgan was quick with the teleportation, but the Dalshie were lightning fast with their black magic.

Later, she would come to the realization that no self-respecting Dalshie would make that much noise while trying to sneak up on two unsuspecting Rengalla, but…

She *wasn't* on her game.

Because some idiotic man had decided to hitch his fate wagon to hers.

"I know it's the bond," she muttered, shaking off his hold, dislodging the strands of magic that had begun to coil around her. "I know the only reason you're interested in me is because of the connection between our powers, and I don't give a fuck. I don't want the bond." She spun, jabbed a finger into his chest. "And I don't want you—"

The rustling increased.

A groan reached her ears.

And...

Out walked the tiniest, cutest little raccoon.

Not a groan. A growl...or maybe a grunt. Or maybe...

An adorable little raccoon sound.

The tiny burglar-mask-wearing mammal scampered forward into the clearing, stood up on its hind legs, and...

Hissed at them.

Darcy startled, jumping backward, tripping over herself, and would have tumbled to the ground if not for Morgan catching her.

"Fuck, that thing is scary," he muttered, his arm wrapping around her waist as he tugged her back a few paces.

The raccoon hissed again.

They retreated a few more paces.

"It's got its beady eyes on us," she whispered as the raccoon stared them down, its teeth bared, that formerly adorable burglar-esque fur seeming very dangerous.

"It's freaky."

"No," she said, still whispering as a trail of even tinier raccoons slid out of the shadows, "*they're* freaky."

Morgan started. "Well, that explains the noise."

Three, four, five...no *six* little raccoons emerged into the clearing, gathered around what Darcy now knew was their mother. And all together, they stared.

And hissed, baring those tiny, razor-sharp teeth.

"Don't those things carry brain-eating parasites?" he asked on a shudder.

"Only in their poop," she said quietly, as they continued to back away, sliding into the tree trunks while keeping an eye on the raccoons.

"Well, they're babies," he whispered. "And babies poop a lot."

Incongruously, she found herself having to stifle a giggle.

Mostly because Morgan sounded so horrified. No. Scratch that. He sounded terrified—as though babies and pooping were the scariest things on the planet.

"Don't be scared," she said lightly, "raccoons use latrines, and that's where the worms hang out."

A shudder. "Don't say worms."

Despite the blood-thirsty animals still staring them down, Darcy found herself grinning. "*Baylisascaris* isn't only a brain worm. It can also migrate to the eye, spinal cord, or other organs."

Mama Raccoon rumbled and sprinted forward a few feet, causing Morgan to tighten his hold and drag her behind him. She could have fought him, could have refused his protection. But hell, all those beady eyes were scary.

Needle sharp teeth.

Creepy feet.

Yeah, she could have done without her night vision adjusting enough to show her those creepy feet.

"How in the fuck is that supposed to be reassuring?" Morgan asked, his magic sliding out of his palms, coalescing into strands that swam through the air and wrapped them-selves around her legs.

"It isn't," she said, using her own magic to erect a shield in front of them. "My point was that there aren't any raccoon bath-rooms around here. So we're safe"—the raccoons lunged again —"for the moment."

"Safe?" he muttered, hauling her backward. "They're going to jump us and pluck out our eyeballs."

"Eye—"

Suddenly, the hilarity of the situation overwhelmed her, and she bent at the waist, giggles bubbling up in her throat. Then exploding out of her mouth.

She didn't realize that Morgan had crouched next to her, that his arm was still around her.

Not until his laughter joined in with hers, a husky rumble that slid over her skin like slightly roughened fingertips, leaving tingling in its wake, raising the hairs on her arms, her nape, gathering moisture between her thighs.

And that was the moment the raccoons attacked.

With a combination of hisses and growls, of grunts and squeals, the posse of raccoons launched themselves at Darcy and Morgan.

She sucked in a breath, readied her magic—

And didn't even have a chance to let it loose.

Because Morgan did.

One moment they were in the clearing, and another they were soaring through the sky, the treetops flashes of black beneath them for just seconds as they tore through the air and away from the killer raccoons.

But not back toward the Colony.

They moved away from it, Darcy just barely able to catch a glimpse of the rainbow of magical strands woven together, protecting her people before they slid through the cloudy sky.

Away and away and—

She found her feet on the ground.

It was colder here, with fewer trees and the cloud cover a little thinner, as though the increase in elevation meant the gloominess couldn't hold as firm against the moonlight overhead.

Morgan was still holding her, and the moment she realized that, she stepped out of his arms.

He let her go...not that there was far *to* go.

They were on a freaking mountain top, the flat plateau he'd landed them on maybe ten by ten square. Though, when she turned, she saw there was a small cave behind her, just big enough to shelter her from the wind that she imagined was quite brisk at this height.

Not that it was blowing that evening.

Instead, it was quiet and still and partly cloudy.

"What are we doing here, Morgan?"

Quiet, then, "This is my place."

She ground the toe of her sneaker into the ground. "What do you mean?"

More quiet. "I think you know."

She did...and she didn't. He was sharing something with her, something she didn't want to know, something that might connect them when she should be running the fuck away.

"This is the place I go to when I need quiet."

A snort. "You're never quiet. You talk all the fucking time. Always *blah blah blah*." She laughed. "It's so fucking annoying." It wasn't, of course. Or at least, not all the time. But it was easier to pretend he annoyed the fuck out of her rather than that she liked him.

Because *that* was dangerous.

He didn't respond for so long that guilt began to weave its way through her.

"Yeah," he eventually said, "You're right."

His tone, so fucking off and sad and dejected and not sounding like Morgan at all, had that guilt *eating* through her. She turned, started to apologize, and got lost in the depths of his hazel eyes—more silver than brown and gold and green in the dim light of the night.

And...she wanted.

"Don't look at me like that, Pem," he murmured.

Darcy blinked, shook her head. "I'm not looking at you like anything."

He cupped her cheek, slid his hand back so that his thumb brushed along her temple. "I can feel this in here"—he tapped his own temple—"in here, remember?" A beat. "I know you didn't mean it"—the bond pulsed in her mind—"so don't worry."

"I'm not worrying." She lifted her chin but didn't bother lying...to either of them. Well, not about the sexual chemistry. The rest of it was fair game to lie about. *That* segment of lying she was all in on. "It's bond-induced attraction," she said. "Nothing about us wanting each other is real."

CHAPTER TEN

Morgan

HE WANTED TO SAY, "It's fucking real. You can't tell me it's not."

But…that would be a lie.

Because he'd stayed away from Darcy for years. Yeah, he'd been attracted to her. Yeah, he'd thought that she was capable and smart. But…it wasn't this overwhelming urge to claim, to drag her into the cave, and to fuck her until they were both seeing stars.

He'd been able to keep his distance…until he couldn't.

Until the bond.

So, he couldn't tell her it was real, couldn't say he'd been pining after her forever.

It *was* the bond.

But…it also wasn't.

The attraction was there, along with the need to claim and make her his. They just weren't the *only* things present in his mind. He also felt her strength in their connection, her sadness, and hidden pain. He could sense the way thoughts flowed through her mind with the rapidity of a flowing river, swollen from recent rainfall. Constant and never-ending. And yet she was able to focus, to forge her way through to the other side.

So much so that no one—including him—ever noticed the turmoil beneath the surface.

As though that river had iced over and was flowing beneath, hidden below a treacherous frozen stretch that was threatening to shatter at any moment.

Yet never actually did.

But he couldn't sense what was causing her pain, couldn't see the actual memories.

Not yet, not until their bond strengthened.

So no, he couldn't tell her the bond was real, that it wasn't because when their magic mixed together, they would create powerful tiny Rengalla.

He couldn't express his undying love for her. He couldn't... give her what she needed.

Which was the reason he'd walked away the first time.

So why was this any different?

Because...he couldn't let her go. Not just because he'd lose his powers, would no longer be a Rengalla if the bond broke, but because...he was starting to know Darcy.

And he didn't *want* to let her go.

"I can't tell you it's real," he said softly.

Her face didn't change, but he felt her wince in his mind, the slight pulse of her pain along the bond.

He snagged her wrist when she would have moved away. "I want to give that to you, to tell you that it's real, and have it be the complete truth. But...I can't." She tugged her arm, tried to free herself, but he held firm. "I can tell you that I like you, Pem. That I liked you then. *That's* what's real."

Her chest rose and fell on a breath. Then, "Why do you keep calling me that?"

No way was he telling her that.

"The bond is here," he said. "There's no running from it."

She scowled—and he felt her thoughts, actually *felt* them.

She was annoyed that he hadn't answered her question, but deeper than that was hurt.

Because he'd left her before.

Because...he'd *hurt* her before.

"The bond is here," he said again, "and it's not going anywhere." A beat. "Unless you want to give up your powers?"

She frowned as she looked up at him. "Of course, I don't want to lose my powers. But"—she ran her fingers through her ponytail, yanked at the end of it—"I don't want someone— *anyone*—in my mind. It's *my* brain, and I shouldn't have to share it with anyone, especially when I didn't allow you in."

"You're right." He followed her when she paced away from him on the narrow mountaintop, the wind whipping her hair around, scattering the strands of her ponytail. Not touching her, even though his palms itched to do so. "But that doesn't change anything, does it?" he asked softly. "We're bound together, and we have to make the most of it."

A snort. "Because, why? You're stuck with me? I'm your cross to bear?"

Her mind pulsed with hurt, with prickly, spiny hurt that made his teeth ache, his brain throb. "*We're* stuck together, Pem. I know I'm not much of a catch." He rested his hand lightly on her shoulder. "Ninety percent of the time, people are annoyed with me."

"That's because you thrive on any type of attention, including annoyance."

His brows rose in surprise. "That's not true."

Except it was.

Being one of three—triplets, no less—and losing his dad at a young age (or young for a Rengalla, anyway), made for limited attention, and he couldn't deny that he'd pestered the shit out of his parents (and then, eventually, his mother) to get more of the focus on him.

Hell, even Francis had told Morgan that he held a PhD in Annoyance Studies.

But now his dad was gone, Francis was gone, and...Morgan was here.

Still pretending that he didn't try to put on a fake façade. Be the funny one because people liked to keep other people around who made them laugh. Be the annoying one because then they couldn't forget about him, because he wouldn't fade into the background. Be the loud, busy, nonstop one because if he *did* stop, then those thoughts would creep in, and he'd start thinking...

And no one wanted him to start thinking.

No fucking way.

Darcy lifted her brows, and he didn't need the link in his mind to tell him that she knew his line was bullshit. He could see it written into the lines of her face, into the pale brown of her eyes, in the pursing of her lips.

She knew it was nonsense, and he braced himself for the tongue lashing she was sure to send his way.

Hell, based on what he'd just realized, he was prepared for the sting that would be unleashed.

He probably deserved it.

No. He *did* deserve it.

But surprisingly, she didn't lash him with insults. She didn't even tell him he was annoying again. She just sighed, fell silent, and glanced up at the stars, now just barely visible.

"I still don't want you in my mind."

"I know," he answered, before realizing *she* was in *his* mind. Or, well, her voice was, anyway. *"I know,"* he repeated, testing floating the words across the bond, knowing that she heard him in *her* mind when she stiffened, her eyes coming to his. *"But we're there."*

Her shoulders slumped, lids sliding closed, chin dropping to her chest. "I know," she whispered.

"And so I can't tell you this link between us is built on love and affection"—not yet, he couldn't—"but I can tell you," he said, *"I can tell you and mean it."* He touched her cheek. *"That I respect you, that I want to build something real, that I want the bond to be real."*

She sighed, didn't answer.

He could sense the turmoil on her side of their link, spinning thoughts that flew so quickly through her mind he couldn't pick apart the individual threads of those spiraling emotions. But he waited. Because he knew that she would come to the same conclusion that he had.

Which was that they were bonded.

They were connected.

They were stuck with each other.

A pulse of something sharp colliding with his brain had him pulling himself out of his thoughts, and focusing back on hers, had him studying her face, searching for a sign that he hadn't imagined that pang.

But his focus only brought him into stilling thoughts, to a placid expression on her beautiful face, to neutral eyes meeting his.

He opened his mouth to ask her if she was okay, but she beat him to any words.

"Okay."

Morgan waited for her to say something else.

But she just repeated, "Okay."

That pulse came again—flared so quickly across the bond and then disappeared just as rapidly—and he went to ask her to explain, to expand, to…say *anything* that wasn't *okay*, but she just smiled, and it was so small and so sad that he stifled that urge to push.

And when she said, "I'm tired," he chalked it up to fatigue and let his protective instincts take over, bundling her against him, wrapping his strands of magic around her, cushioning her from the speed of the transport before teleporting them both back to the Colony, just outside the shield.

They passed through, walking side by side to her quarters.

Then paused, just outside her newly repaired door.

Pale brown eyes, a rosebud mouth, tendrils of hair escaping her ponytail to curl around her cheeks. Unable to stop himself, he reached forward and tucked one behind her ear.

And was drawn in.

To her scent. To her body. To her mind.

She wavered. In her mind. In her body, drifting close to his.

Then...she straightened, calmly set her hand on the lock, and murmured, "Goodnight."

It wasn't nearly enough, not when he wanted to push her back into her room, to make love to her until the worry and hurt and fear had disappeared, until he didn't feel any more pulses of pain, any more spiraling thoughts.

But...it was also enough.

Because she wasn't retreating. There weren't steel plates in his brain keeping him out. Nor fury being lobbed in his direction.

Just caution.

And he could understand that completely, could respect that just as much.

So...he didn't reach to smooth back those other tendrils, didn't talk his way into her rooms. Instead, he just stepped back, nodded, and murmured, "Goodnight."

Then waited for her door to *click* closed, for her footsteps to disappear down her hallway, and then, keeping one eye on the bond, he found his own bed.

But even with those steel walls down, it still took him a long time to fall asleep.

CHAPTER ELEVEN

Darcy

THEY WERE STUCK with each other.

She slid down the wall, allowing the hot water of the shower to flow over her, pushing all her concentration to plaster over the bond, to coat it with placid thoughts, hiding the pang of pain.

This was her worst nightmare.

She didn't want a deep connection.

Because intimacy wounded. It hurt and destroyed and… made her feel like she was small.

You.

It's your fault.

You're pathetic.

I wish you were dead instead of her.

Said so many times after her mother had been killed in a Dalshie attack, killed protecting Darcy, killed in a way that meant her father—never the most stable to begin with—had deteriorated, had blamed her, had…

Made it so that she'd hardened her heart, built barriers around herself.

Self-fucking-preservation, but that didn't mean it was any easier to have the vitriol lobbed her way until she was old enough to get out, old enough to move to the Colony and start training with the other soldiers, old enough to be on her own and reckless and to take missions...

Like the one tracking Daughtry before she'd come to the Colony, befriending her, trying to discover if she was the girl who'd been kidnapped as a child, her magic stifled.

Spoiler alert: she had been.

But during that mission, Darcy had finally felt like she'd made a friend, a good friend...but one that had been built on a lie, and so...it had become one she'd lost.

Rightfully so.

Because Darcy had lied to Dee, and even though they'd patched things up, were politely friendly, trust like they'd had couldn't be rebuilt, especially when its weak foundation had been because Darcy was hiding a really big truth.

The one time she'd followed mission orders to the tee, wanting to finally be promoted, trying to be a good soldier and in doing so, was willing to put her morals on the line.

Never again.

Fuck being a good soldier. She'd question what needed to be questioned. She didn't have much left in her life, and if she couldn't look herself in the mirror and know she'd done her best to do the right thing, then she didn't have anything left.

And now she was bonded to a man who wanted nothing to do with her.

Or all the things he *wanted* with her had to do with their magical connection and not losing his powers, no matter the pretty words he wanted to toss her way.

So now she had to decide.

Was she going to run? Was she going to give it all up?

Or...was she going to accept that she was going to always be someone's last choice, their worst-case scenario, their...burden?

"You're kidding yourself," she whispered, slamming her

palm to the tile, still careful to keep her emotions under wraps, lest Morgan feel them. "You're always going to be someone's last choice, and you're going to accept it because you don't have any other choice."

And that was the truth.

She wasn't going to give up her magic, stop protecting her people.

That was the one thing she had.

So...she'd take whatever crumbs were tossed her way, accept her fate as someone to be *stuck* with, and she would take Morgan as her bondmate.

No matter if it shattered her to pieces deep, *deep* inside.

———

SHE WAS ready for the knock.

She couldn't say that she'd slept a whole lot. But she'd slept enough to be ready for her perimeter shift. Slept enough that she was awake when she felt Morgan's presence growing in her mind, telling her he was coming toward her as effectively as a homing beacon.

And his emotions were even more clear that morning.

Eagerness and apprehension.

If only Darcy's emotions were as simple.

Because she had a fucking whirlwind going on behind the calm mask she was exuding.

But she'd made her decision the night before. She was going to nurture the bond. She was going to accept the connection she had with Morgan. She was going to deal with the lot the universe had handed her, and put her head down, and get through it.

Perhaps it wasn't the most romantic of sentiments, but...it was honest.

It was truth.

It was reality.

She opened the door, saw that handsome face, those beautiful eyes, and her heart hurt. But she'd had a lot of practice hiding hurt, hiding herself. So, she smiled and said, "Good morning," and felt his beat of pleasure.

"Hey, Pem," he murmured. "Breakfast?"

"I have an early shift."

He held up a bag. "I know," he said. "I'll walk you out, and in the meantime, you can eat this." He pulled out a wrapped bundle, and the smell assaulted her nose.

In the best way possible.

Bacon and eggs and cheese.

"I—" She shook her head. "It's not Tuesday."

Morgan shrugged one shoulder. "Lex"—the Colony's head chef—"owed me a favor." He held out the sandwich, then took her hand and folded her fingers around it when she didn't immediately grab it. "Eat, baby."

A shudder along the bond.

From her.

One she barely caught and blocked off before it slid across her side of the bond and toward Morgan. She took a breath, thought of her special spot, the one that never failed to bring her peace and calm when she remembered it.

Saving up for the plane ticket to Turks and Caicos.

Staying at a hotel that butted right up onto the beach.

The sounds of waves crashing through her open windows, the sticky ocean air on her skin, blowing back her hair.

Feeling like she could breathe for the first time in her life.

That was what she sent down the bond. The calmness she felt when she had been on that tropical island, life seeming so simple.

Sand and sun, breeze and bright blue water.

Her lungs unstuck, and she took the sandwich, peeled back the paper, taking a bite so she didn't have to speak.

But she'd forgotten about the bond—okay, she hadn't forgotten, but she'd forgotten about the whole being able to speak across their link thing.

Which meant she jumped when she heard his voice in her mind—*"You sleep okay?"*—and her strategy of cramming her mouth full of egg and bacon and cheese backfired almost immediately as she jumped, inhaled, and promptly began choking on the huge bite she'd taken.

A warm hand resting between her shoulder blades, sliding up and down her back gently.

And just like that, her body relaxed in some sort of Pavlovian response to the big, lightly stroking palm.

"There you go, Pem," he murmured as she managed to chew the bite and swallow, this time without choking. "There you go."

Soft voice. Softer hands.

"Eat, baby."

She found herself obeying. Partly because of the command that came both aloud and in her mind and partly because the sooner she finished this sandwich, the sooner she would be over the risk of choking.

On the sandwich at least.

Because Morgan was the kind of sexy that could make a woman choke on air.

Especially when he smiled.

Or walked beside her with all his liquid strength barely contained, his sweet and spicy scent drifting through the air.

Or spoke gently into her mind again. *"Did you sleep okay, baby?"*

Thankfully, she hadn't taken a bite at that moment—so there wasn't anything to choke on. "I slept fine," she said, not daring to speak along the bond, not ready for that yet. "You?"

His hazel eyes came to hers, held for a long moment. "I slept fine."

And...they lapsed into silence.

She wondered where the carefree joking man she knew had

gone. She didn't know how to handle this quiet, contemplative one who brought her breakfast sandwiches and asked how she had slept.

A teasing inflection about *what* she'd slept in, yes.

This? No.

It made her tongue-tied and unsure and had her stuffing her face with her sandwich.

Eat. Walk fast. Haul ass to the outside of the Colony and get some space, some fresh air.

A tug on her hair. *"Hey, why did the ketchup blush?"*

She didn't choke this time…even though the intimacy of his mind brushing along hers felt like her skin was being rubbed the wrong way…and also the right (?) way. She knew that didn't make a lick of sense, especially because beneath that mix of wrongness and rightness was a persistent tug.

To strengthen the connection.

To pull Morgan into a broom closet, kiss him within an inch of his life, and then welcome his cock inside her body. Welcome it because it was big and glorious and brought her pleasure. A *lot* of pleasure. Or…it *had*. Because maybe that pleasure, that sexual tension had been easy. Nothing like the complication of the bond. God, if she could just have the physical, leave the emotional behind, and…things would be simpler.

She sighed inwardly, knowing that it wouldn't be.

But part of her did wonder if perhaps this newfound tension and hesitancy would mean that they'd never be as explosive as they once—

Fingers on her nape, pushing her ponytail to the side, warm lips and hot breath on her skin. "I asked you a question, baby."

She sniffed, slid away from him. "You *asked* me nothing," she snapped. "You *gave* me a stupid fucking lead-in to a joke I really don't want to hear the punchline to."

"You sure?"

Was she sure?

Darcy wasn't sure about *anything*. She was a mess and trying to figure out a way forward that wouldn't destroy everything inside her.

So, she shoved the last bite into her mouth. "Yes, I'm sure," she said, pretending the only thing on her mind was the bad joke that was sure to follow.

"You *sure* sure?" he asked, tugging her hair again as they strode through the front doors of the Colony, pushing out through the heavy pane of glass, moving toward the shield. She was due to run the green course, to patrol one of the more heavily wooded areas—and hopefully not coming in contact with any of the rabid raccoons. "Stop thinking about raccoons, Pem, and tell me you want to hear my joke."

Irritation boiled through her, and she turned and slammed a palm against his chest. "Get out of my head."

He covered her hand with his palm, bent so that his lips were a hairsbreadth from hers. His eyes blazed. "*No.*"

CHAPTER TWELVE

Morgan

MURDEROUS THOUGHTS WERE TRAILING down the bond, flowing from her mind to his.

Maybe most men would have been terrified of all that rage focused on him, the sparks of magic—of *Bond Magic*—but Morgan liked Darcy when she was full of emotion, when she was strong and fiery. Literally.

The sparks were coalescing, forming into small flames that licked over her skin.

And he couldn't deny that he fucking loved seeing her covered in his magic.

Yeah, he was an alphahole.

No, he didn't care.

But even more than that spark inside her, he really fucking hated the cool distance, the placid calm hiding what she was feeling beneath. *Ms.* Darcy might think that she was fooling everyone, fooling *him* with the faux composure, the taciturn distance, but he was in her mind. He could sense the emotions beneath, even if he couldn't quite ferret them out.

Yet.

That would come in time.

The important thing was that he'd won the first battle, convinced her to give them a shot. She wasn't running. She'd eaten the food he'd brought her, and he hadn't found the linens, the candle, the painting in the hall.

Darcy was letting him take care of her.

At least a little bit.

So, he was going to keep doing that. Continue to take care of her, continue to push a little at a time, gain her trust, and win her over, dammit.

Even if he had to do that by annoying the shit out of her.

Because, as everyone knew, he was really good at that.

"Why did the ketchup blush?" he asked again, the words out loud and along the bond, because—fuck it—he could do both and the more he spoke into her mind, the more she would get used to him there, the less it would be a threat, especially when it was communicating for the purpose of stupid fucking jokes.

Her pale brown eyes came to his, fire in their depths. Her palm on his heated, and he smelt the fibers start to singe.

Then her lids closed, her shoulders rose and fell on a breath, and the warmth faded. "Why?" she asked—only aloud—her tone more than begrudging. It had slid straight into resigned.

Victory!

He brushed his lips across hers, straightened before she could react, and said, "Because he saw the salad dressing."

She froze.

Then dropped her chin to her chest and sighed loudly.

Then something wonderful happened.

Her shoulders relaxed and laughter filled the air, slid across the bond. It was...fucking glorious. Then she stopped, their gazes connected, and she surprised the shit out of him by rising up on tiptoe, slanting a kiss across his lips—a not gentle, not sweet kiss. A kiss that had plenty of tongue and heat and had his cock going instantly hard.

She pulled back, whispered in his mind, *"I'll bring you dinner, Trouble."*

Then she was gone.

Striding across the lawn, slipping through the shield, and disappearing out into the forest, her dark brown hair fanning out behind her.

But her mind, the bond, their connection...

It was stronger than ever.

"ARE we just pretending we're not talking about this?" his friend asked.

Cody was leaning against the back wall of the armory, directly behind the stall that Morgan and Mason were using for target practice.

Unfortunately, Morgan knew exactly what Cody was talking about.

Namely, the fact that they'd been out on the training field up until about twenty minutes ago, and Morgan's magic suddenly wasn't just *his* magic.

His brother had recognized the change immediately— Mason's eyes coming to his, and he had practically been able to hear his brother's surprise registering in his mind. That's what came from being a triplet. Their connection was tight.

But Mason was quieter than Morgan. He'd given Morgan a look that screamed they would be having a conversation later, but he'd left it at that.

And considering that Darcy's magic was a pale brown that fit right in with his gold, green, and slightly darker brown strands, he had thought he might have a bit more time before having to navigate this conversation....and the gossip train of the Rengalla.

Sigh.

He picked up his gun, aimed at the target, and fired.

Until the magazine was empty.

Which was far too soon.

Another sigh and he set down the gun, turned back to face his brother and his friend and knew that gossip would be flying in a matter of minutes.

If it wasn't already.

Who was he kidding? It had probably been flying from the moment he'd used his magic out on the field.

"Who?" Mason asked.

"It's your turn to shoot," Morgan said, nodding toward the stall.

But his brother didn't move to pick up his gun.

And Cody, who wasn't even there for shooting practice—and not even bothering to pretend like he was—was just standing there, staring at Morgan with a huge smirk on his face.

Probably because Morgan had made it his mission to give his brother and Cody and the other bonded males so much shit that they were eager to return the favor.

It was just...he had about a fucking tissue paper's worth of trust built with Darcy.

He didn't want to fuck that up.

"Who?" Cody repeated.

"It's none of your fucking business," Morgan muttered, grabbing another magazine and shoving it into the bottom of his gun.

There was silence.

And then...laughter.

Loud, riotous laughter.

That Morgan knew he deserved, even if he wasn't going to acknowledge that fact. He just slapped on his ear protection—which didn't drown out the laughter, the fuckers—and unloaded the gun into the target.

Head. Heart. Head. Heart. Trying to shoot through the same holes as much as possible.

And failing.

Because he knew he was about to be given some shit, and it was shit he deserved, because he was the biggest shit giver of them all.

The last bullet flew, sailing several inches off his target.

He wanted more bullets…he wanted more time to delay the inevitable.

But he didn't have either.

Sighing, he took off the ear protection, set them on the counter, and took care of unloading the gun. Mason didn't step up to take his turn, and Cody didn't either. They just stared at him, arms crossed, a single eyebrow raised, and waited.

Ugh.

He hated when people tried to outwait him.

Mainly because he was never patient enough to outwait *them*.

Cody switched eyebrows—and seriously, Morgan couldn't even lift one by itself, let alone switch between them.

"Darcy," he said before they could ask *who* again.

Now he had four brows raised and two sets of wide eyes staring back at him.

"*Darcy?*" Mason exclaimed, "but she hates you."

Morgan snorted. "It's not that bad." When Cody made a sound of disbelief, he narrowed his eyes. "I won't say that Dee was your biggest fan, or Suz Graham's, or Alex John's."

"The difference is that my Dee didn't have a chip on her shoulder the size of a Mack truck."

A bolt of annoyance shot through him, but before he could say anything, Mason added, "And Gabby was soft, bro. Darcy is a graveyard surrounded by barbed wire. You say the wrong thing, and you're going to get impaled…and then tossed into an open grave."

Okay, first of all, this was his bondmate they were talking about.

Second of all, they didn't fucking know her.

Not that he knew her. Well, he was working on changing

that. Because there was a whole wealth behind her walls. He'd barely gotten a glimpse of it, but he knew that Darcy was hiding something beautiful and fragile beneath her rough exterior.

Misjudged.

She'd spent far too much time being misjudged amongst her people, pushing everyone away like she was a frightened, wounded animal.

And he'd missed it.

Missed that.

Missed that she'd gotten worse after he'd broken things off between them.

Because he'd been too wrapped up in himself and his promotion.

Fuck he was an asshole, and he opened his mouth to tell Cody and Mason just that when he felt it.

Felt *her*.

His gaze slid from his friend and brother down the hall and to the woman who'd made a home in his heart. The woman who was holding a platter of food, her skin shimmering lightly with a layer of Bond Magic—an identifier that made it impossible to hide that she'd bonded.

More alphahole bond bullshit, as Suz always called it.

Evolutionary measures to warn other men away, at least until the bond settled and it disappeared, thoroughly satisfied that the woman was secure.

And fuck, that *was* some alphahole bond bullshit.

Morgan knew it was a miracle that no one had noticed the layer on her yet. A miracle that had been helped by the fact that she'd spent most of the last two days away from everyone in the Colony.

But now she was standing ten feet away from him, a tray in her arms that said she'd been in the cafeteria—and that Bond Magic covering had certainly been spotted, and paired with his training in the gardens and Cody and Mason and…

Yeah. Word was out.

But that was the smallest worry in his mind at that moment.

Because Darcy's face and the flash of pain lancing the bond for just a millisecond before it was replaced with that placid calm he was really fucking starting to hate were the biggest ones.

Her chin came up. Her eyes went hard and flinty. "Gentlemen," she said, moving forward and setting the tray down on the table that ran the length of the back wall of the shooting range. "Hope you all are hungry."

Then she spun.

And was gone.

CHAPTER THIRTEEN

Darcy

SHE GOT AS FAR as the door to the armory before she slowed, took a deep breath, and clamped a hand over her heart.

Her eyes burned.

Tears were a heartbeat away.

But…

Fuck it.

She was tired of running away, tired of feeling hurt, tired of…feeling like an outsider.

So, she didn't think or consider or do any of the things she'd trained herself to do from the moment she'd decided to stop fucking around and to truly devote herself to being a soldier. She spun on her heel, pushed back into the armory, and began marching back down the hallway toward the stalls where she'd overheard the men talking about her and her prickly nature.

And the chip on her shoulder.

And the barbed wire.

And the open graves.

God, *that* one hurt. Because she'd been trying so hard to be seen as valuable, as a productive part of the Colony, as someone who could be respected...and still, they thought she was...well, a total bitch.

That hurt.

It was unsurprising.

But it still hurt.

But she was tired of taking that hurt, tired of running away and hiding that hurt from the people who'd inflicted it.

The men—two who'd said things that sliced, one who hadn't spoken and because of that sliced even deeper.

Morgan was supposed to be her bondmate, supposed to protect her, and what had he done? Brought her a sandwich and bought some trinkets from Target.

Yes, they were new.

But no, he hadn't stuck up for her.

And because he was inside her, because they were connected in a way that she hadn't wanted but was there anyway...that stung worse than what Cody and Mason had said. Because she'd spent her day convincing herself it was a good idea to keep moving forward with her plan to accept the bond despite the likelihood of getting hurt—and seriously, who would have thought that hurt would come so quickly? Because despite the knowledge of that impending hurt, she'd had a little slice of hope.

Just a sliver that was brewing.

Because he'd come after her the night before. Because he'd known her favorite breakfast, and he'd brought it to her without strings.

Because...she wanted it.

The happy ending. The adoring mate. The...one person in the world who would love her for her.

They were deep in conversation when she approached, Mason's hand clamped down onto Morgan's shoulder, Cody standing close.

"Give her some space," Mason was saying.

"Fuck that," Morgan said. "I have to go after—"

She stopped, straightened her shoulders. "I know I spent a lot of time being difficult," she said, forcing the words to be calm but firm, even when the three of them spun to face her. "I know that I pushed back when I should have been a good soldier who just followed orders. But I've learned and have gotten better, and I'm not that same girl who showed up here a few decades ago. I've worked my ass off to be a valuable addition. I've put my life on the line, and I've done good work." She swallowed hard, words coming faster and louder when Cody opened his mouth to speak. "I know you're my superiors, but seriously, fuck you. Fuck you for talking about me behind my back. Fuck you for judging me by the person I was instead of who I am now—"

"Darce—"

She turned, glared up at Morgan, and strived for calm. "And fuck you. Because you tell me you want to build a future with me, but then you turn around and complain about being stuck with a woman like me." Now her voice cracked. "I didn't choose this. It's not my fault that we've bonded. And if you truly feel like I'm such a heavy burden to bear, then we should just call it now."

Morgan's face clouded; his mind spun against hers. "That's not—"

Darcy ignored him and turned to face Cody. "I know you probably hold a grudge against me because of my behavior with Daughtry. It was never my intention to hurt her, but I know that intentions don't matter. *Truth* matters. *Reality* matters."

Cody's green eyes flashed with guilt. "That's—"

"So, I'll keep working on being a good soldier. I'll keep fighting for our people." She slid her gaze to Mason, who knew what it was like to lose people whom he loved, who had lost his wife, his child. "I'll fight the Dalshie if they return. I'll fight whatever other threats appear. But I won't fight for simple respect. Not any longer."

"Baby—"

She turned back to Morgan, feeling her eyes burning again, her throat going dry. Her placid calm that had been covering her end of the bond was completely gone, dissipated like so much smoke. "I know I'm not what you want. I know I'm not sweet and soft." She sucked in a breath, released it slowly. "But when you've been hurt over and over again. When you've lost everything and been told you were worthless and unwanted more times than you can count, soft isn't there. Concrete is. Steel and barbed wire and open fucking graves are. So...take it or leave it."

Then she turned and walked away.

And made it all of three steps before Morgan caught her arm, mind blazing against hers, his grip tight. "I'm taking it," he said, anger and regret twisting along the bond. "I'm taking it, Darcy."

She laughed, but it wasn't filled with the least bit of humor.

"I'm taking it," he said again.

"Right," she told him, tugging her arm free. "I guess we'll see if that turns out to be true."

———

SHE WAS IN THE KITCHENS.

It wasn't her shift, but it was late, and she couldn't bear to sit in her empty rooms, the painting on the wall, the candle on her desk, the quiet in her mind.

Because that was the bond.

Quiet.

Distant.

Quiet.

He'd said he was taking it...and quiet.

So, she was making of that what she could. Meaning that she was going to live her life, and that would either be a life where she'd have a bondmate, or it would be one where she didn't have any powers and she lived as a human.

If it was the latter, she had a bit of savings.

She'd pack up, buy a house on an island that was surrounded by clear blue water, and live her days out with the ocean air blowing through her hair, along her skin.

For now, she was scrubbing at these blackened pots like they were her enemy and her only job was to get them shining again.

"You know that I have a dishwasher for just this purpose," Lex said.

She glanced up, leaving her hands—and wrists and elbows—in the pot, her fingers gripping the sponge. "I don't mind doing it by hand."

"This newfound elbow grease of yours have anything to do with the Bond Magic currently coating your skin?"

It had everything to do with it.

But she wasn't going to admit that.

"Nope."

Lex hopped up on the steel table—something that he would ream anyone working back in the kitchens for—sighed and crossed his arms. "Of course not." He shook his head. "Instead, you're going to waste all my sponges and get your hands all pruney and—"

"You're going to get clean pots and not complain about it."

Lex's lips twitched. "There is that." A shrug. "Well, definitely the first, maybe the second. I really like complaining."

"Yeah," she muttered. "I know that."

He fell silent.

She kept scrubbing.

"You know I'm happy for you, right?"

She'd been working the pot in an even pattern, scrubbing from the right side to the middle, then the left side to the middle, shaving off part of the circle with every pass she made. But Lex's words had her freezing.

No.

She didn't know that.

Wasn't sure she believed it...except that Lex wasn't one to put any effort into lying, and he certainly didn't have a polite bone in his body.

He said what he meant, and it was as simple as that.

"Right," she whispered, then added, "Thanks."

The pot flew out of her hands, water splashing up her front, but just as quickly that damp moisture was wrung out of the material, a ball of water held in place by Lex's magic spinning in front of her. It gently sloshed into the sink, flowing down the drain, leaving her with damp hands and a sponge that would do no good.

Except the sink was dirty, so she began scrubbing that.

Just to give her hands something to do.

Lex sighed but caught the pot that was still half-filled with water, using his magic to send the remaining liquid down the drain, then hopped off the counter, turned the large metal cylinder over in his hands, and used air magic to carry it through the kitchen as he tugged open the door of the dishwasher and loaded it on the heavy-duty rack inside.

When he turned back and saw her still cleaning the sink, he sighed again.

But he didn't return to the steel counter, didn't hop back up and tell her to stop scrubbing. Instead, he went to the fridge and pulled out several pans. From some, he scooped the remains into the compost bin, others he moved into a few large, lidded containers. One, he served up onto a plate, topped with ice cream, and, by the smell of it, his famous hot fudge.

A hand on her shoulder, squeezing lightly. "Eat first"—he held up the plate and she saw that he'd put together a decadent brownie sundae—"then I've got more pans for you to scrub."

She smiled. "My therapy, you mean?"

A nudge. "Your therapy is the sundae and the wrinkled hands. The side benefit to both is that I get clean pans."

Somehow, she laughed.

He nudged her again, coaxed her into grabbing the plate. "Eat, Darce. Then clean up as much as you want."

Her heart squeezed.

"Hell, if you're feeling ambitious and not in too much of a sugar coma after that sundae," he said with a grin, "I think that the freezer can use a deep clean."

She laughed again, and Lex smiled his big, lopsided smile.

Another squeeze, happiness flowing through her, and she found herself picking up the plate with the brownie sundae, scooping up a large bite, and eating until she was in that sugar coma.

And then she washed the plate, the fork, the pans…and deep cleaned the freezer.

Her wrinkly hands were totally worth it.

CHAPTER FOURTEEN

Morgan

HE WANTED to be anywhere but here.

He *wanted* to be with Darcy, explaining and winning her over and taking away her hurt.

But it was his turn to be here.

Here being the LexTal's command center.

Running surveillance on the exterior of the Colony.

Because some fucking humans were camping, and it was intruding on their space. And while the humans couldn't see beyond the glamour that hid the Rengallan stronghold, if they happened to make it through the shield and past all the feelings of unease and "Go away" that they had woven into the magic to keep humans out, the Rengalla would be in trouble.

Hidden but separate was the best policy.

Because when they intervened with humans, the humans tried to take advantage, or they got jealous, or...they got hurt.

Which, unfortunately, was looking more and more likely was going to happen in this instance.

The dumbasses were heading toward the gorge.

Where the rocks were slippery from the waterfall that

sprayed regularly, where the sun had gone down, and the magic had been laid thick to make the space even darker than normal. Which…when it came to these dumb ass teenagers who were daring each other to jump off the cliffside…

In the dark.

In the cold.

Fucking morons.

"Fuck," Tyler hissed as a stupid group of teenagers egged each other on toward the edge, ignoring all common sense and instinct.

Because they were teenagers.

And none of them wanted to look like pussies with their girlfriends.

But, more than likely, one of them was going to end up dead.

"I've got them," Morgan muttered, pushing out of his seat and hauling ass for the exit. He was at the shield in minutes, pushing through the strands seconds after that, his mind immediately going to the bond, checking in, feeling for Darcy even though it was almost painful to touch their connection.

The calm was gone.

The bond ached and throbbed instead.

She was hurting, but he was here, chasing down some teenagers because it was his *turn*. Fucking assholes.

No, *he* was the asshole.

Because she was right. He hadn't protected her, hadn't spoken up, hadn't—

Hell.

Not the time. Closing his eyes, he took a breath, concentrated on the location, felt his magic well up and surround him. A breath. A push through the air…

And he was in the shadows behind the group of cocky males.

No, not males. Boys. Naw, older than that. Man children.

Man children with a death wish and hard dicks that were

desperate for the girls they were with, even though they'd be lucky to get to first base, if they didn't strike out.

"You go first."

Nervous laughter. "Naw, you first."

Scuffling feet. "Don't be a pussy."

Now the girls were giggling.

"Do it, Robbie," one of them called. And seriously? Not even the girls had any common sense?

"Yeah, Robbie. *Do* it!"

Nope. Not an ounce of smart amongst the group of them.

"Max, this was your idea—"

More scuffling, a sound of alarm, and with a sigh, Morgan stepped out of the shadows. "Want to tell me what in the fuck you're doing on my land?" he asked, leaning back against a tree trunk, his arms and ankles crossed.

The girls spun around with a squeal.

The guys turned and backed up, dangerously close to the edge now.

"Come away from there!" he snapped, wondering when in the fuck he'd stopped fighting black magic and immoral monsters and started wrangling teenagers.

The boys jumped, but instead of moving away from the danger, they skittered back toward it.

And this was not going to end well.

He straightened off the tree when one of the boys slipped and the girls squealed again. *Fucking hell.* There was nothing to it, he was going to have to use his magic…and then he'd have to get Tyler to wipe their minds.

"Hey."

The soft voice had made him jump, but on the contrary, it seemed to calm the kids.

"Hey," Darcy said again as she slid out of the trees behind him.

He hadn't felt her. He should have, should have sensed her approaching. But he hadn't, and now she was here and not looking at him. Instead, she was solely focused on the group of teenagers, her movements slow and steady, her voice calm.

If he couldn't feel the throbbing pain in her brain against him, he would have thought she was completely unattached.

"I know it's scary to have people come up behind you in the middle of the night," she was saying, still careful, still steady, "but the edge of the waterfall is slippery, and there are rocks at the bottom. You don't want to fall...or jump."

A note of chastisement.

Enough that the boys moved forward, safely away from the edge.

"Now," Darcy said, "are you going to walk out of here, or do I need to call the police to escort you off our property?"

Their faces paled, but none of them processed the lie— neither Darcy or Morgan would ever call the police, and if for some reason, hell froze over and they did call the human authorities, it would take them hours to get up the hill in order to do anything about the trespassers.

The only reason the teenagers were here was because they were camping in the regional forest—illegally—and had been steadily making their way toward the boundary of the Rengallan land.

Hence the surveillance.

Hence the interference before they got too far.

"We didn't know," one of the girls began.

"We know," Darcy said, her voice going gentle again. "Which is why I haven't called them yet. So, why don't you come away from the waterfalls—and promise me you won't make a habit out of jumping off them...at night...when you don't know anything about the pool at the bottom"—she fixed the teenagers with a look, and they all straightened, nodded quickly—"then walk back down to your campsite and make sure that next time you know where you're camping."

"We-we'll go."

"Also, there are bears and cougars"—*and rabid raccoons*—"out here, so you'll want to be careful where you *do* camp."

"B-bears?" one of the boys said.

"And most of the property owners out here don't take kindly to trespassers," she added. "If you don't come across a bear, you're likely to be on the receiving end of a shotgun."

Silence.

Then, "We'll get out of here and won't come back."

That was the smartest thing they'd said from the beginning of this entire interaction.

"Okay"—Darcy gestured down the path—"then you'd better go before it gets any later."

More nods. More shuffling, though thankfully this time it was away from the falls and down the trail. Darcy watched them go for a minute and turned to him. "Make sure they go all the way out." Then she spun, started to head back to the Colony.

"Pem—"

"No."

She didn't turn around. Just told him *No* and continued walking.

"I'm—"

"Do your job, Morg," she said.

"You were magnificent," he blurted.

Her feet stuttered for a moment before she continued walking, disappearing into the trees, her voice dropping in volume as it drifted to him along the bond. *"Don't worry about me. Just... do your job."*

———

HE KNOCKED on her door a few hours later.

But he knew the room was empty before his fist finished rapping against the metal panel.

The bond was stretched taut, pulled until it felt fragile.

Distance.

There was a lot of distance between them.

He took a breath to calm his mind. Exhaustion rippled through him. Too many nights with too little sleep and too much stress.

He was supposed to be charming. Women liked him. Hell, he was friends with most of his exes (and polite, at least, with the others, Darcy having fallen into that category before this shitshow of a situation). Shitshow because he never seemed to be able to do or say the right thing when she was around, because he was so far off his game that he was fucking up with her left and right and…

Totally at a loss for how to fix it.

Hell, he'd happily forget fixing it. He'd accept just not taking a hammer to her heart every single time they were together.

Sighing, he turned away from the door, the bag with the sandwich he'd managed to coax Lex into making two mornings in a row—even though Lex always said that he wasn't "a fucking short-order cook and didn't do special requests"—crinkling (Spoiler alert: he *did* take special requests. He was just grumpy and snarly when he did).

Then he went to the surveillance room, intent on locating her with the cameras (yes, it was an invasion of privacy, no, he didn't care).

John and Cody were sprawled in the chairs, eyes on the monitors.

Cody cut a glance toward him, regret written into the lines of the face. "She's not here."

He'd known that, *felt* that, but he'd hoped…hoped that he was wrong. "Where?" he asked.

Cody shook his head. "Tyler marked her as going through the shield and again at the waterfall with you and the kids." He clicked some keys on the laptop in front of him. "But he didn't log her coming back into the shield, and she hasn't shown up on any of the perimeter cameras either."

Because she'd had her own quota of surveillance shifts and knew where they were.

Knew them well enough to avoid them.

His heart squeezed in worry, but he pushed through that.

The bond told him she was alive.

She wasn't hurt...or not physically, anyway. Because the emotional pain along their connection was receding, less throbbing and more occasional ache. Calm was trickling back in— and as much as he hated that, he was glad she wasn't hurting quite so fiercely.

But that realization didn't clue him in to where she was.

Luckily, he had a built-in Darcy detector.

CHAPTER FIFTEEN

Darcy

SHE WAS SITTING on the porch, contemplating arson.

Again.

Never let it be said that she couldn't cycle and spiral with the best of them.

Because she'd gone inside and she'd seen that piece of blue ceramic, the empty shelves, the worn cabinets, and she'd cried.

Like a baby.

Like a big, ol' baby who was hungry, or who had lost her favorite toy, or had a dirty diaper, or—

Whatever else made a baby upset.

The shard of porcelain was in her pocket, digging slightly into her thigh through her sweats. Her hair was piled on top of her head, covered by a beanie and a baggie hoodie that was more thin cotton than warm material.

And she was watching the sun come up, wondering if she should turn the house behind her into ashes.

Or if she should leave it as a reminder of the past.

So as not to forget.

Because...she shouldn't forget.

"Right," she muttered, pushing off the steps and starting for the car she'd signed out. Arson would take too much effort. Better that she just let the place rot, like the remaining memories she had. Except, "Like I'm *going* to forget."

"Forget what?"

The voice in her head had her whirling around, seeing Morgan standing amongst the trees, having assumed the same position she'd watched him take the night before—ankles crossed, arms crossed. The only difference was that his lips were turned up into a smile.

Her mind slid to the bond, to the connection she'd been studiously avoiding. She should have noticed it getting stronger with his proximity.

But…it was beginning to feel normal.

Yes, how much she could read through the bond came and went depending on how far apart they were, but it also didn't feel like some sort of alien invasion any longer. It felt…right.

It felt…fluttery.

She felt fluttery just looking at him.

No. She hated him. She *should* hate him. But…instead, part of her just felt relieved that he was here, that she wasn't alone, that he might understand and—

Go her.

Sign her up for the Glutton For Punishment Club.

Good times.

She might as well burn her feminist card while she was at it.

Treat me like shit and my heart flutters.

And maybe my eyelashes too, just so I can convince him to like me and love me and—

Her magic roiled under her skin, but not as fiercely as the disgust. So fucking needy. Just like her father said. It exploded out of her fingertips, coiled around her arms.

Such a needy bitch.

Except, that voice wasn't her own. It was her father's.

But the gentle hands…*those* weren't her fathers or her own.

They were Morgan's, and part of her hated herself for enjoying the way they felt when they rested lightly on her shoulders, when they tugged her against him.

"Darce—"

She stiffened, bracing herself.

"I'll help you burn it, if you'd like."

She pushed off his chest, mouth dropping open.

He gave her a lopsided grin, shrugged as he called forth his own magic, hazel flames coiling around his hands.

"But why?" she asked.

"Something in there hurt you," he said.

She nodded, not sure why she didn't deny it, but...she didn't deny it, just gave him that small piece of herself, a test of sorts.

"And"—his fingers grazed her cheeks, the flames dancing over her skin, not burning her. Instead, they were as intimate of a caress as if he'd dipped his fingers between her thighs—"I've been doing a shit job of protecting you from things that hurt you." A breath, his voice going light, his mind nuzzling against hers gently. "So, a few correctly placed flames wouldn't be remiss."

Turning, she studied the worn porch, the cracked panes of glass in the front door, the yard that had once been filled with pots of colorful flowers and was now overgrown.

"I don't want to burn it," she whispered. "Not yet, anyway."

Those fingers were gentle again, this time drifting across her nape. "Okay," he said, and his magic dissipated, sliding back into his palms, banking in his mind. But his body didn't leave hers, the heat of him on her spine, his scent in her nose. "Do you…"

She glanced up.

His cheeks went pink, just a little bit at the edges, and his mind brushed tentatively against hers. "Do you want to go for a walk?" He nodded over her shoulder, and she turned to look. "Maybe down that way? We can—"

"No!"

She stumbled back a step. "No," she repeated, "I—" A breath, struggling for calm. This wasn't then. Another breath. God, so many years had passed since it had happened, and she was safe. She was older. *In. Out. Calm, Darcy. CALM.* She was stronger. She could protect herself—

Her throat went tight.

"Breathe," Morgan ordered gently.

She couldn't.

Her lungs weren't working. Or maybe her brain wasn't.

Or maybe it was working too well, too fast, too—

Images flew through her mind.

With her mom in the workshop. Her mom sitting at the wheel, forming a vase while Darcy worked on a sculpture of a sheep, using a toothpick to add texture to the wool.

Her favorite raspberry-scented candle burned on the table.

Pale blue ceramics lined the shelves.

"You're so talented, baby," her mother said, the wheel spinning as her hands, covered in mud-colored clay, worked. Her magic twined through the clay, nudging it this way and that, showing off her talent. Effortless and beautiful and so much better than Darcy's sheep.

But her mom always made her feel good.

Her mom was the nicest mom in the whole world.

The radio was playing in the background, a song that had her tapping her toes and her mom singing along to the chorus.

And then a crash.

Her mom's hands stuttering, jerking, and drawing a large gash through the formed clay.

"Oh no," Darcy began.

Another crash.

Her mom froze, and she reached up, switched off the radio, leaving a smear of clay on the knob.

"Wh—"

"Shh." Her mom stood up from her stool. "Come here—"

The door to the workshop blasted open—wood splintering, glass shattering, pottery exploding into a million pieces. One piece flew through the air and sliced the top of Darcy's hand, blood squirting out and dripping down her skin, and she watched in shock and horror as it dripped down onto a broken chunk of a blue-glazed plate.

Tears filled her eyes, but she barely had time to react, not when her mom was grabbing her arm, dragging her toward the windows. She pushed one open just as a strand of black magic sliced through the workshop, a rotten smell filled the air. "Run, baby," she ordered, throwing up a wall of magic, its deep brown threads shining brightly. She shoved Darcy through the opening. "Run deep into the woods to the creek. Find the purple flower, pull it, and hide inside."

"But Mom—"

One more push and Darcy hit the dirt.

"Go, baby."

Darcy stood up, reached for her mom's hand. "But—"

Her mom's magic had begun unraveling and she teetered on her feet, sweat running down her temples, her skin going pale. "Run, Darcy. Run now. Don't look back."

Darcy ran.

But she looked back.

She saw her mother's magic fail.

Saw the Dalshie step into the room, horrible magic crackling as it filled the space, the carapace, insect-like skin gleaming in the sunlight.

Saw the spiked strand of black power fly toward her mother.

Heard the thud of her head hitting the floor.

A scream tore out of her throat—

"Baby. Shh, baby. Shh, it's okay," Morgan was saying as the memory cut off, his hand sliding up and down her back. "You're safe. I'm here. You're safe. Just breathe."

It took her a minute to do just that, to inflate her lungs to release the extra air, to…breathe.

Then it all seemed to click, and she was able to inhale and exhale again.

"Did you…" Another breath in. Another breath out. "Did you see all of that?"

"Your mom?"

She nodded. "Yes."

He pushed back the hair from her face. "Yes, Pem, I saw it."

"I—" Her heart was racing. Her eyes burning. She didn't like to think of that day, of what happened afterward.

"My dad was killed by the Dalshie, too."

Calm words, but his mind was completely open to hers, and she could feel his pain, sense the tumult of his memories.

He was hurting, too.

He was...*hiding*, too.

"What happened?" she whispered.

"A mission went wrong," Morgan said after a moment. "They were pinned down, and he teleported everyone out, but...he took a bolt of magic to the heart and...he was gone."

"It doesn't seem possible that it can happen that fast, does it?" she whispered. "That with the flick of a wrist, one strand of power, and they're...just gone." She snapped. "In a second."

His throat worked. "It doesn't seem possible, no."

They fell into silence.

Then Morgan asked, "Do you want to go somewhere? Somewhere that's not here," he hurried to add when her gaze drifted down that path toward where that terrible memory had taken place. "Somewhere away from here."

"Are you going to trap me on the top of a mountain again?"

His lips twitched. "That's only for very special occasions."

"Like freezing your bondmate's ass off?"

"Like taking her someplace so she'll have to cuddle up to me."

She weighed the words against the bond, against his mind tucked into hers, and knew he wasn't lying. Morgan wanted her near.

Her. Not someone else.

Maybe he hadn't been happy with her, but she couldn't lie and say she'd been happy to be linked with him. Not at first.

Because now…well, she was cautiously optimistic. He'd tracked her down. He'd held her and shared.

And he wasn't running.

Maybe he hadn't stood up for her, hadn't repudiated what his friend, his brother had said. But she didn't need a champion. She had her own back. She'd fought to find her own spine.

She didn't need a man to swoop in and save the day.

She had herself.

That was enough.

It would have to be.

CHAPTER SIXTEEN

Morgan

HE'D MANAGED to get through an entire evening without hurting her.

Low bar, he knew.

But Morgan was going to take his victories where he could get them.

Now it was the afternoon of the following day, Darcy had been working in the kitchens, and he'd been off-site with John, scouting old Dalshie hideouts—and finding none of their old enemies. John and his mate Alex, Daughtry's sister and a slender soldier who'd met John at the front entrance with a long kiss, had both followed him into the space...where their trio had nearly mowed down Darcy.

Who was carrying a large platter of sandwiches.

"Whoa," he murmured, snaking an arm around her waist and tugging her close, using his other hand—and a bit of air magic—to steady the platter. She'd gone stiff at the contact but softened when he bent his head and kissed the side of her neck. *"Where are these going?"* he asked along the bond, noting the stiffening, noting that another kiss had her softening again.

"To the," she began, and then he felt her mind brush against his. *"To the gardens. Kids are having a picnic."*

He snagged the platter. *"You have anything else to bring?"*

A nod toward the basket on the edge of the cafeteria counter. "I just have this and the dessert."

He didn't miss that she'd retreated from the intimacy of the bond's telepathy, but she'd given him a little bit, and that little bit was more than he deserved, especially since he could practically feel her bracing herself, holding her breath, expecting that John and Alex would say something negative about her or their relationship, such that it was.

Which they did.

It just wasn't…what Darcy clearly expected.

And it wasn't negative. Or about their relationship.

It was about a different one…Alex's newfound love affair with junk food of every type (she'd grown up without a lot of extras, including junk food, and John had made it his job to give her every single extra he could think of…and, no surprise, she loved chocolate).

"Did Lex make his brownies?" Alex asked, excitement in every line of her body.

More bracing from Darcy, and then she shook her head. "He was too busy with prepping for dinner. I…um…I made them."

Alex whooped. "Can I have one?"

"I…well, I don't know how good they are," she said.

"Is it chocolate?" Alex asked.

Darcy nodded.

"Then I don't care how good they are."

A beat before Darcy's lips tipped up, a tendril of humor trickling along the bond. "Then," she said, waving a hand toward the basket of baked goods, "I guess I don't care if you have one."

Alex grinned and fist-pumped, loping over to the covered serving dish, peeling back the plastic wrap, and grabbing one of the palm-sized brownies. "You didn't skimp on size, did you?"

Her brows waggled, and Morgan felt Darcy's humor and confusion all twined together through their connection.

It was fascinating and beautiful to watch, especially when she didn't close herself off to him.

Progress.

They were making progress—so long as he didn't fuck up.

Alex was still waggling, and eventually, Darcy settled on, "No, I don't" as a reply.

Which gave Alex her desired effect. Because she chuckled, nodded approvingly, took a bite, then moaned. Loudly. "Oh my God," she said through a full mouth of chocolate goodness. "You're a goddess, Darcy. An absolute goddess."

"I'm glad you think so," Darcy said, but she was smiling. She moved to the platter, pulled out another brownie, and plunked it onto a napkin. "But now I've got to get the food to the kids before they start a revolt."

"Go, go," Alex said, waving a hand. "I'll just be here enjoying my baked goods."

A nod and a tentative smile as she picked up the platter. Then she turned back to Morgan, held out her free hand. "I... um...I have to take that one, too."

"I know, Pem." He kissed the side of her neck again, straightened slightly and murmured in her ear. "I'll come with you."

She shivered, fingers clenching on the plate. "I can manage on my own."

"I know," he said again. "But I'll still come with you."

"I—"

A tug of her hair. "Kids. Restless. Remember?"

She nodded, turned for the door. "Right."

"Pem?" he asked along the bond.

Slowing of her feet, a glance over her shoulder. "Yeah?"

"You look really beautiful today."

She slid to a halt, and he brushed by her, pushed open the door, holding it wide for her. "Let's go feed the beasts."

Wide eyes, warmth in her mind.

He'd take it.

He'd fucking take it.

———

"THIS ISN'T EXACTLY what I meant when I said I want to take you for a date," he said two nights later.

Two days without fighting.

Two days of tentative thawing.

Two days without hurting her—without anyone else hurting her.

Progress.

She slammed the magazine into the gun, cocked it. "You've been bragging about your shooting skills for *years*," she teased. "It's about time to show them off."

He waggled his brows. "I'd rather show something *else* off." A beat. A nip of her ear. "Something I remember that you liked very much."

"If *I* remember correctly"—humor drifting across the bond —"you bragged about your shooting skills before, and they were a bit...premature..."

Pre...

He gasped in mock outrage. "How dare you?" he growled, sweeping her up into his arms and away from the weapons. He spun them, glad the armory was empty this late at night, so he could plunk her on the table at the back without worrying about any interruptions...or anyone screaming about their eyes being scarred.

Fucking brothers.

Fucking friends.

"Why are you cursing your friends?" she asked, her hands dropping to his shoulders and holding him away from her.

He nipped at the inside of her elbow, drew her close.

And the best part?

She let him.

Whether it was the bond or their past or the fact that he hadn't fucked up in the last few days, he didn't know. He was taking it, and he was running with it, and he was reveling in the fact that the woman he wanted was in his arms and allowing him to touch her, and—

"Ow!" he exclaimed, rubbing the side of his neck.

"How does it feel?" she said pertly.

"I don't bite you."

Her brows lifted, and he remembered he'd just nipped *her*.

"I don't bite you on your throat," he amended. They rose again. "Fine. I don't bite you *hard* on your throat."

She smirked. "Oh, Morgan, you're so full of shit," she teased, laughter bubbling up in her throat, and the sound was so wonderful that he froze.

Then she froze.

And braced, careful calm coming to the surface.

Fuck.

"You can tease me," he said gently.

Darcy's eyes drifted over his shoulder. "Right."

"In fact," he said, lifting a hand and cupping her cheek, turning her head so that she was looking at him again. "I like it when you give me shit."

"Right," she murmured again.

"Pem." Her eyes had been drifting again.

They came back to his. "Yeah?"

"I know I haven't inspired much trust, but...look, baby. Really look into my mind and *see* what I feel for you."

She rocked back, her head shaking slightly. "I—"

"Just look." A beat. *"Be brave, Pem. Just one more time."*

It was too soon to do this, to push, to pressure her, but they had a roadblock in front of them that wouldn't be removed until she *knew*, until she believed, until she trusted.

And for her to do that, he had to be wide open.

"Morgan," she whispered.

"Please," he whispered back.

Darcy inhaled, released it slowly, and then...she *looked*.

CHAPTER SEVENTEEN

Darcy

SHE'D DEALT with a lot of shit over the years—some of her own making, plenty from her father, a bit from other people who didn't understand her.

But *this* shit?

This shit terrified her.

Because Morgan meant something, he always had, and the few slices of his thoughts that he'd allowed her to overhear... well, they hadn't felt good.

Stuck. Together.

She took a breath.

Released.

They *were* stuck together, and it was better that she know everything, could deal with it, because she wasn't running from the bond, from Morgan. It was better to be prepared, to face the problem head-on, and—

She *looked*.

Closing her eyes and allowing her consciousness to be drawn along the bond, floating through her mind and into Morgan's.

It was…strange.

She didn't have telepathy, had purposefully kept to her side as much as possible. But this…she wasn't sure if it was what telepaths felt, or was uniquely for people who were bonded, because it was the strangest—and most wonderful—sensation she'd ever experienced.

A breath.

Then being immersed.

Completely immersed in a sense of rightness, as though she were coming home for the first time since her mom had been killed, warm arms wrapping her into a hug, holding her tight, making her feel safe and secure and—

Things shifted, the fog cleared slightly, and she dropped into his mind a little deeper.

Regret made her recoil, want to retreat into the safety of her own brain.

But she wasn't a coward. She needed to know it all.

Darcy allowed herself to sink a little deeper into his consciousness, allowed the tendrils of his mind to wind around her, to keep her close.

"*Look, Pem,*" he murmured.

A deep breath and she studied that regret, understood finally what it was about. Her eyes shot to his, and it was strange that it somehow brought more intimacy when she was already so intimately connected to his mind. But it did, and… she fell deeper.

Able to see beyond the regret, beneath it.

To the tentative hope beneath, the urge to protect, the need to be with her.

Since she felt that same pull, it was easy to process—that was normal bond nonsense.

But when she went to retreat into her own brain, she tripped over another tendril, this one large and pulsing and…

Hot.

It wrapped around her ankle and sucked her down as

quickly as a whirlpool, yanking her beneath the surface of his consciousness and revealing...*need.*

A raging need that tore through her like an elephant running through a piece of tissue paper.

"I—"

"Easy, Pem," he murmured, stroking a finger down her cheek, his mind wrapping around hers, tugging her back up to the surface. "I've got you."

He did, pulling her out of the torrent, guiding her back into her own mind.

And it was a good thing because Darcy was...*on fire.*

Desire had torn through her, filled her every nerve and cell. It compressed her lungs, shortened her breathing, made her skin feel like it was three sizes too small. Heat slid down her spine, coiled in her stomach, gathered between her legs.

"*That's* what you feel?" she whispered incredulously.

His mouth turned up. "A bit of it."

"*All the time?*"

Her words slid along the bond without effort, without thought and damn, that felt good. Felt *right.*

He tugged her hair. "All the time, gorgeous."

"But...wait...a bit?" More incredulity. More shock. Because if that was a *bit*...holy shit, she couldn't imagine what more than a bit would be.

The man bopped her on the nose. On the *nose.* Then grinned.

"Morgan—"

"God, I like it when you say my name," he growled, nipping at her throat again and making her giggle. *Her.* Giggle. Like seriously, how? She was Darcy. She was a badass with a demeanor of steel. She didn't giggle. She glowered and challenged and—

Another nip.

Another giggle.

That was...unfathomable.

While she was still reeling from that, his hands came to her waist and lifted her down.

"Let's shoot."

Giggles.

Gunshots.

Her life didn't make sense anymore.

————

HE WAS WAITING outside her door.

Like he did every morning.

A bag in hand.

Not always with a breakfast sandwich—today's was a donut —because Lex wasn't always inclined to play short-order cook.

But he was there.

And…she liked it.

Look, she knew that she was supposed to like it, that was the whole point of the magical connection. To bring two people together who were compatible.

She just didn't think she was going to like it this much.

Which was a little terrifying. But she was *used* to terrifying. It would just be a little bit easier if she were confident in her ability to keep a little bit of herself back. That was the part that had been changing over the last week.

The bond was growing.

Her resistance was waning.

And Morgan…was perfection.

Perfection she wasn't confident she could accept.

"Sleep okay?"

She nodded.

They fell silent, and this was the part she wasn't confident she could accept. Because even though they were silent, it wasn't uncomfortable. And who in the hell was comfortable in silence? It didn't make any sense. They should be talking as much as possible, discovering every single thing about each other…

Except…she already knew.

She was in his mind, and he was in hers.

He knew about the breakfast sandwiches and the raspberry-scented candle.

She knew he was addicted to coffee and that it was probably part of the reason he never seemed to run out of energy.

Well, that and he was Morgan.

He never looked tired, not even this morning after they'd stayed up late last night, just sitting and talking in one of the common areas. She'd thought briefly about inviting him back to her rooms to watch a movie, but…she didn't have any movies.

Or a TV.

Why?

She hadn't needed one. Why again? Because she had spent a lot of the last years punishing herself.

Because she'd left her father, who'd spent the previous years punishing her.

Because she'd thought she deserved it, thought she should have done something to protect her mother…even though she couldn't protect herself.

And because she'd believed the words that her father had shouted at her time and again.

Believed the words he'd written her on his deathbed, one final *fuck you* and blow to her confidence that he'd carefully orchestrated.

Before he'd died.

Not at the Colony, but at one of the satellite bases, having refused to come to any place where she was.

Like she was a plague, a dark mark, someone to be avoided at all costs.

Now he was gone.

But his legacy and the memories lived on.

She sighed inwardly, breathed through the pain, and then

tugged Morgan to a stop, opening her mouth, preparing to ask him to go somewhere to talk, to lay this out there. Because she was done with letting the past overwhelm her. But his face was placid.

Too placid.

And that was when she felt him in her mind.

Her brows rose.

"I'm sorry," he said quickly. "I felt the burst of pain, and I looked down the bond. I shouldn't have. I—"

"Did you hear what I was thinking?"

He winced. "I—"

Her eyes slid closed, and she focused on the bond, on his feelings, on what he was thinking. As always, there wasn't any artifice.

Just Morgan.

Hating that she'd been hurt, empathizing that she'd lost her mom, wanting to rage at her father, even though he was already gone.

"Well, you finally know what was in the letter, don't you?"

Another wince. "I'm sorry. I didn't mean to hear. I'll figure out a way to give us some privacy—"

"It's okay—"

He didn't seem to hear her, just kept talking. "I shouldn't have pried. I know that's on me, know how important your privacy is to you." Contrition flowed across the bond. "I'll talk to Cody. I know that he has a way to shield so that they have some separation, and—"

"*Morgan.*" She waited for him to look at her, to halt the flow of words, then covered his hand with her own and smiled, feeling lighter than she had in years. "I'm not upset."

Brows dragging down. "You're not."

"Check."

More brow dragging.

"Look and see, honey," she said, then added along their connection, "*Look across the bond.*"

"I—"

"*Look.*"

He looked. His presence was like shrugging into a warm coat, sitting in front of a blazing fire with a mug of hot cocoa, sinking her toes into soft, white sand.

"*You're not mad,*" he whispered along the bond.

She shook her head. "Plus, look at it this way," she said lightly, "I guess that will save us some time in future conversations, won't it?"

He relaxed, mouth curving up, and flipped his palm over so they could interlace their fingers. "I'll still find out a way to make sure you have privacy—"

"You need privacy, too," she pointed out.

"I don't." He bent, brushed his lips over her throat. "I don't need anything except you."

Her heart squeezed, but she didn't retreat.

Instead, she trusted.

With their fingers linked together, they started walking forward. "Well, I can say one thing about the bond," she said as they turned the corner for the hall that led to the gardens—since she had a shift with the primary students that morning...something that Morgan knew without her having to tell him, something that fed the trust between them, that cut off her terror in its tracks.

"*What's that?*"

She could do this.

Darcy smiled. "*It doesn't suck.*" A beat. "*Not completely, anyway.*"

Morgan glanced at her then his lips twitched. *Then* he burst out laughing.

And it was the best sound in the world.

Because she knew.

She knew that she really, *actually* could have a real relationship and be her *real* self, and not fuck it up.

CHAPTER EIGHTEEN

Morgan

HOT WATER SLUICED over his skin.

His head hung forward, chin against his chest.

He was tired. It had been a long day, with several group teleports that had required a large amount of power, almost so much magic that he was nearly tapped out.

It was trickling back in now, slowly refilling his reserves, but it would be hours before he had the strength to teleport again.

Teleporting might be out, but he always kept enough power for self-defense. Still, it wouldn't be much of a defense because he was a dumbass and had pushed too far because he wanted to get back before Darcy left for her shift—

Good thing he was going to come right back and pass out for six hours.

He was showering quickly then going to run to the cafeteria to bring Darcy some breakfast—or dinner, really, since it was six at night, but it was going to be breakfast for her since she was on the night shift.

He didn't like her out in the dark by herself, but...she was a soldier, and it was her turn for that patrol route, so he'd walk her to her sector...and he'd walk her back to her rooms in the morning to make sure she got some sleep the next day.

See?

Even though the bond was riding him, making him desperate to wrap her in cotton and put her on a shelf where she would be safe and he could protect her, he *could* be reasonable.

And watch the bond, even while he was sleeping.

Yes, that was an oxymoron. No, it wasn't a lie. His body was so in tune with hers that she began breathing heavy and he was at full alert.

Speaking of breathing heavy...he was doing plenty of that himself.

Waking up hard and aching, desperate to take the next step with Darcy. He knew how good it had been between them in the past, but now, with the bond, being able to feel what she felt, having that strong connection, and he was...well, desperate for that next step.

He was, of course, also desperate to prove himself to her— hence the holding off on the claiming portion of events.

It was fine.

He was fine.

He was old enough to temper the driving need inside him to claim.

Though, ignoring that urge was getting harder every day, probably why he was also acting old—or maybe *young*— enough to jerk off in the shower.

Repeatedly.

Multiple times per day, every day. In the shower. In his bed. At his desk.

Dreaming about lightly calloused feminine hands brushing his aside, stroking him firmly. Or better yet, coming around behind him and taking him deeply into her—

He groaned, tilted his head back, and gave into the need,

wrapping his fingers around his cock, gripping it tight, and jerking it hard and fast.

Quick.

Quick.

So he had time to take care of her.

Pale brown eyes, lush pink lips, breasts that fit perfectly in the palms of his hands, a pussy that—

The shower door slid open.

He spun, his hand still on his cock, his eyes flying open, magic surging in his mind, shooting forward and—

Stopping.

Because Darcy stood there, hair pulled back into a high ponytail...

And nothing else.

As in, she was *wearing* nothing else. His brain short-circuited, fingers tightening on his cock, pleasure shooting down his spine—*her* pleasure shooting across the bond, mingling with his, sending him to the razor's edge of control.

He dropped his hand.

"Don't," she whispered.

He blinked.

"Don't do that." Another whisper, but this one was accompanied by her stepping forward into the shower, the mist gathering around her body, droplets glistening on her skin. She reached for his wrist, her fingers covering his as she wrapped their hands around his cock. "Do this," she murmured, stroking their palms up and down. "Do *this*."

His breath shuddered out of him; pleasure coiled at the base of his spine.

"Fuck," he hissed.

She pulled her hand away, but her gaze stayed glued to his cock. *"Do it,"* she ordered along the bond. *"Make yourself come."*

As if he could stop.

As if he could deny her anything.

As if...

Fuck.

It didn't take long. It didn't take more than three strokes.

One. Two. Fucking Tootsie Pop.

He blew, cum shooting out of his cock, painting itself across her abdomen. Pleasure tore through him. Not gentle in the least, but in a fucking tsunami that burst out of his brain and flooded his body, a second wave just as strong impacting him from Darcy's side of the bond.

She stepped toward him, wrapped her arms around his waist.

"Your shift," he said, when he could finally breathe again, think again, move his limbs again. "I got your hair wet"—the stream of water was shooting over his shoulders, cascading down his chest, and soaking her where she leaned against his torso—"and you need to go outside and work. You'll catch cold."

She rubbed her nose back and forth across his middle. "You don't catch a cold from your hair getting wet," she said lightly. "But I don't have to go out for my shift. Steven asked if I could trade with him and cover his tomorrow." Morgan frowned. "Apparently, he has a big date with Elena."

His arms tightened around her, and he buried his face in her hair. "Are you tired?"

"I'm not the one who just came," she said pertly, leaning back to meet his gaze. "Are *you* tired?"

His cock twitched. "What do you think?"

"*I* think that the man who had my palm print coded to his lock, who was all but calling me to him with sexy images of him jacking off in his shower, will have the energy to make good on those fantasies circling through his mind." She rubbed her hips against his. "I particularly like the one with your mouth on my—"

He'd stopped thinking about five minutes before she'd even gotten into the shower with him.

He could barely pull two thoughts together now that he'd had an orgasm.

But her mention of his mouth on her spurred him to action.

He wrenched the water off, scooped her up against him, and shoved open the shower door. A second later, her ass was on the vanity counter, his knees were on the rug in front of the sink, and his mouth...was exactly where he'd been dreaming it could be.

On a pussy that tasted like ambrosia.

Her desire coated his chin, filled his taste buds, had his cock going hard all over again. Because it was every bit as good as he'd expected. He could feel her pleasure in his mind, and it tangled with his, ramped his until he could barely see straight, until... every time he did something that made her feel good, his desire ramped higher, desperate to be inside of that tight, wet heat.

Not just his tongue, his fingers.

He wanted his cock pounding deep, wanted to feel her muscles clenching tightly around him.

Wanted—

"That," she moaned into his mind. "Yes," she gasped aloud. "I want that. I want you inside me. I want—"

He redoubled his efforts.

No way was he going to take advantage of her, push too quickly. No way was he going to give himself another orgasm without getting her off first.

"Okay, yes—right there—" Her head *thunked* back against the mirror. "Orgasm first and then you giving me another orgasm while you're inside me second."

"Greedy," he thought, and her laughter rippling across the bond, through his mind had him thinking that telepathy was handy. *"I like it."*

"I like it, too," she thought huskily, *"and I like it right there. Yes. God. There!"*

He focused on that motion, focused on her pleasure ratcheting higher, her orgasm coming closer. Her thighs clenched around him, her hips jerking as she ground her pussy against his face, sweat broke out on his spine, and his cock was mere seconds away from exploding. He reached a hand down, gripped it tightly, and redoubled his efforts, sliding his tongue deep before sucking hard on her clit and—

Her moan was loud and long, and her orgasm sent pleasure scouring his veins.

"Fuck," he whispered, after he'd slowly brought her down, bringing his own control back from the razor's edge incrementally. Gained enough control so that a gentle breeze wasn't going to make him come.

"Right?" she whispered, lifting her head. "That was…"

"Incredible."

Her lips curved. "Yes. *Incredible.*"

He stood, and she looped her arms around his neck, bringing her breasts very close to his mouth, the fucking minx. As such, he couldn't resist dipping his head, nipping her someplace new. She released a breathy moan, pressed her breasts, and then he was scooping her up, carrying her into his bedroom, dropping her onto the mattress.

"Now that I know what you like," he said, crawling down over her, stopping to press kisses at all his favorite spots— which was basically everywhere from the smattering of freckles on her forearms to the curve of her collarbone, to the dip of her belly button, to the narrow thatch of hair between her legs, to the glistening and pinked folds of her pussy, "let's do that again."

"Or," she said, wrapping her legs around his shoulders and flipping him.

In a movement he allowed, one, because she'd surprised the shit out of him and totally got the drop on him, and two, because that flipping of his body got her sitting on his face, and…

Yeah, he was down with that.

He was down…literally.

He clamped his hands around her waist, yanked her pussy against him, and ordered along the bond, *"Ride me, baby."*

Pink on her cheeks.

Embarrassment and desire through her mind.

He flicked out his tongue, danced it over the bundle of nerves…and the shyness faded away. She bucked. He sucked. And then moisture was coating his face, her head was falling back, and—

"Oh God," she moaned. "Oh God. Oh God. Oh *God."*

It was tempting to answer with his usual line of *"Yes? You called?"* But Morgan was a grown-up, and he was with the woman he wanted above all else, and he didn't want to bring his usual snark to the occasion. Not when this was important and meaningful and—

"I heard that," her light voice trickling along the bond.

He nuzzled her thigh. *"That this is important and meaningful."*

"No." A beat. *"Well, yes. But also"* —she slid down his body— *"for the record, I like the snark. I like…"* A breath, her eyes coming to his. *"I like you."*

Her hips brushed his, her pussy slid back and forth over his dick.

"I…I like—"

She sank down.

And he lost his mind.

CHAPTER NINETEEN

Darcy

ONE SECOND SHE WAS MOANING, her body stretching around his cock, pleasure and pain mingling through her center as she slid down on him, and the next…

She was flat on her back with Morgan's lithe, muscled body over hers, and he was pounding into her.

It was glorious.

It was almost too much.

It was…*glorious.*

He bent, his mouth slanting across hers, his tongue fucking her mouth in time to his thrusts, and she went from turned on to molten.

"Slow. Slow. Slow."

Since that was definitely not what she was thinking—she was thinking *faster, harder,* and *Oh God, yes, right there*—it cleared her mind a little bit, allowed her to focus enough to realize that Morgan had completely lost control and was trying, rather desperately, to regain it.

Well, she didn't want that, didn't want him all buttoned down and restrained.

She wanted him wild. For her, for them, for their connection. But mostly for her.

Which was why she wrapped her arms and legs around him, leaned up and slanted her mouth across his, and said, *"No. Faster. Harder. More."*

His eyes opened, locked with hers.

"Give me everything," she demanded.

His hips had slowed, his hands fisted on the comforter.

"Everything," she whispered, breaking the kiss. "Everything, baby."

A flare of emotion.

Heat in his eyes.

Then the final thread snapped.

He was everywhere, in her mind, in her body, touching and stroking, pounding and kissing, nipping and licking.

Completely out of control.

And she fucking loved it.

But she especially loved that she could feel everything *he* was feeling, how it mixed with every sensation cascading through her body, how it made her head spin in the best way and her heart pound, and her body shiver with delight. She absolutely reveled in the fact that she knew exactly how much he loved the way she felt, the way he cataloged every moment —the color of her hair in the dim lights, the way her breasts bounced as he pumped into her, the feel of her legs around his hips, how her neck arched when he hit a particularly good spot.

And the way he pounced on that.

How he concentrated on exploiting that location.

Over and over and *over* again.

That was good. *Really* good. Really fucking good. And she forgot about Morgan's cataloging. She forgot about seeing herself as he saw her. She forgot about the swirling thoughts and the ever-growing bond.

She was lost in the moment.

In the pleasure.

In Morgan.

A gasp as he had her teetering on the edge of that fall into pleasure.

"Come, Pem," he murmured into her mind. "Come for me, baby."

And she did.

Not because he ordered it, but because he hadn't stopped moving, because he was still hitting that spot, because…it was fucking perfect.

Explosion.

It was too much…and perfect…and too much…and—

Morgan groaned, falling over the precipice beside her.

And…perfect.

Yes, it was absolutely perfect.

———

HE WAS TALKING to the men.

The ones who didn't like her, who compared her to barbed wire and open graves.

And…she wanted to go say goodbye.

Because he was going reconnoitering and she had the day off, and then she would be on the day shift starting tomorrow morning, and…so they wouldn't see each other for two whole days.

Which felt like an eternity.

Because they'd been in this lovely bubble for nearly a month, and she was worried.

That things were going to change.

It was easy to pretend they weren't when the man was sexing her into blissful nirvana, giving her orgasms left, right, and center…and in the shower, the bedroom, against the wall, and in one broom closet that she was going to fondly refer to as *their* broom closet.

But now, when he was going away with his friends instead

of being sequestered with her, glued to her side, bringing her breakfast, and sleeping in her bed—or *his*—and…

Her courage was failing her.

She wanted to just walk up to them, to kiss him goodbye, and—

"Hey."

She blinked, turned, and saw that Morgan's brother had come up behind her. Mason had the same hazel eyes as his siblings, but his hair was shorter, his demeanor quieter.

"Hi," she said cautiously.

And silence.

She cleared her throat, allowed her gaze to drift over his shoulder, waited for him to say…*something*.

But nothing, and when she finally couldn't stand the tension, she started to turn away. "I should just—"

"Stay," he said.

Darcy blinked. "Um, what?"

"Stay," he repeated. "Morgan will want to say goodbye to you." A beat. "Especially since two days apart is like torture for a newly bonded couple. He'll need you close."

"As an open grave?" she asked tersely.

Yeah, it was petty.

Yeah, she should have let it go.

But that wasn't her, and so…she'd just said it.

Mason winced. "I'm sorry. I shouldn't have said that. I was worried about my brother and…" He trailed off, probably realizing that didn't sound much better.

"It's okay," she said.

"It's not."

"You're right," she agreed. "It's not. But I shouldn't have brought it up again. You're his brother, and you were looking out for him. I can't…" She shrugged. "I can't be upset for that."

"You should be."

She jumped, turned, and saw Cody.

"What you said to us in the armory," he said. "You were right."

"I—"

"No." He touched her shoulder. "I spent the majority of my life being an asshole." He bent a little closer, dropped his voice. "And feeling like an outsider. I know what it's like to push everyone away when what you really want is to have people close. To have people love you and make you feel like part of their family." He squeezed her arm. "I know that because I lived that, and I should have recognized that you needed that, too."

"It's not—"

"On me?" He straightened, tugged the end of her ponytail. "It is, and I'm sorry for it." Another tug. "And I promise to do better."

"I—"

"Hey. Hands off my girl." Morgan's tone was joking, but she felt the coil of possessiveness pulsing along the bond.

Which Cody apparently picked up on, because he backed away immediately, putting a few feet between them. "We'll let you two"—he cleared his throat, probably because Morgan was now giving serious (and overt) possessive vibes—"say your goodbyes." He glanced at Morgan. "Departure in five minutes."

Morgan nodded.

Cody walked away. Mason started to follow, paused, and met her eyes. "My mom has invited you to dinner tonight."

Darcy choked. "What?"

Mason chuckled. "That's the problem with bonding with a triplet. Lots of family to contend with, including an overbearing mother-in-law." He grinned when she choked again. Nodded as he said, "Mom expects you tomorrow at 6:30 sharp."

Her mouth dropped open, and she started to say…*something*.

But what was there to say?

Once, the idea of dinner with a man's mother would have

terrified her. But Matilda had raised Morgan—and Mason and Monroe—and he (and they) were all pretty great.

"Pretty *great?*" Morgan asked.

"*I'm having dinner with your mom?*" she countered.

"You don't have to go," he murmured, wrapping his arms around her and tugging her against his chest.

And seriously, nothing felt more right than that.

Which, based on the smirk sliding through the bond, the stink knew.

"Don't think that I missed all those possessive vibes you were putting off, mister," she grumbled, still plastered against his chest, knowing that staying cuddled up to him meant that she was totally belying her words and not giving a damn.

"I wasn't asking you to," he said, slanting his mouth over hers. *"You're mine."*

She sputtered, pulled back. "I'm *what?*"

A bop to her nose, another kiss to her lips, her throat. "Mine," he repeated, nipping the sensitive skin there. "And I'm yours. And"—his tongue darted out, soothed the slight sting—"I love you."

Darcy froze.

He pulled back, reached forward, and cupped her cheek. "I love you, Darcy. It's not the bond or your fabulous body—though I love both"—he grinned—"I love the person you are inside. I needed you to know that before I left." His expression and mind went serious. "Just in case, I need you to know that I feel so lucky to be bonded to you, to be able to know you, to be allowed to love you."

It seemed like all she was doing was sputtering and choking and scrambling for words.

So, she spoke along their connection. *"Is...is this mission something more than reconnaissance?"*

His arms came around her again. "No," he murmured, inhaling deeply. "But I don't ever want you to doubt how I feel about you."

"I—"

She wanted to say it back.

Wanted to be able to just blurt it out.

But…she just didn't have it in her. Not yet.

He tugged her ponytail, smiled widely. "It'll hold, Pem," he said gently. "It'll hold."

"Why do you call me that?"

He stepped back. "I need to go."

She narrowed her eyes. "Morgan."

Humor along the bond, mischief in his mind. "Love you, Pem, and see you in two days."

"*Morgan,*" she growled.

"Darcy," he countered. "My quiet, snarly, taciturn *Darcy.* I think you need to do some reading while I'm gone."

A kiss floated along their connection.

A smirk on his handsome face.

Then he was walking backward, his magic crackling as it filled the air. "*Bye, love.*"

Her heart pulsed as she watched him bring it around John, lifting them both off the ground, Mason following suit with Cody.

They started to disappear, and Darcy's heart squeezed.

And the words…they just came.

"*I love you,*" she whispered along the bond.

But Morgan was already in the air, zipping away faster than her eyes could track, putting so much distance between them so quickly that the bond strained like a taut rubber band.

And she didn't know if he heard them.

And later…she would really wish that she knew for sure that he had.

CHAPTER TWENTY

Morgan

HE RELEASED HIS MAGIC, grinning when John stumbled slightly on the entry, looking far too green for a man who'd teleported with regular frequency.

"You need me to hold your hand?"

"Fuck off," John muttered, sucking in a deep breath. He released it slowly and some of the green faded. "Let's go," he grumbled, when Mason and Cody landed, the latter looking even more nauseated than John had.

"I hate teleporting," Cody grumbled, bending and resting his hands on his knees. "Fucking hate it so much."

Mason reached into his pocket, pulled out a plastic-wrapped package of saltines.

He tossed them to Cody, who caught them reflexively, took one look at the contents and then crushed them in his palms. "Real funny," he muttered, shoving the ruined crackers into his pocket. "Let's get this done. We still have three more to clear, and I want to get home sometime this century."

And just like that, they were serious.

Ready for this.

Morgan sucked in a deep breath, released it slowly. Then brought his gaze up and scanned his surroundings, knew that his brother, his friends were doing the same. But the space was quiet, nothing but insects buzzing and wind sliding through the trees.

They approached the empty building, a former factory that was so rundown it looked more like pieces of wood held together with string than an actual building.

But it was one of the few remaining nests they hadn't cleared.

So, they needed to go inside the structure that should have been reduced to ash, make sure there weren't any Dalshie left, make certain they'd done any necessary recon...and then they'd reduce it to ash.

Get in.

Get out.

Get back to their bondmates.

———

HE DROPPED the piece of wood back down to the floor—or the remains of the floor, anyway—and sighed.

"I fucking hate small spaces," Cody muttered.

They were pondering the hole that led down to the basement of the building, its stairs looking like jagged teeth, the darkness and shadows heavy and oppressive, which weren't helped by the fact that the sun had slid behind the clouds, giving the entire area an ominous feeling.

His nape prickled.

He pushed the sensation away.

"I never knew that," Morgan said, forcing his tone to be light —made easier when he reached out and touched the bond, reassured himself it was still there. He couldn't telepath Darcy from this far away, but he could feel that she was alive and well, and that was exactly what he needed to get through this mission. "You need me to hold your hand?"

"Fuck off," Cody grumbled, punching him hard. "It's Dee's fault. She's scared of small spaces and somehow that transferred to me. Probably because it's fucking terrifying to feel your mate's fear." He shook his head. "It's a whole other playing field to have them be scared. It does something to your heart and mind—" A sigh. "The bond is the best thing that has ever happened to me, but sometimes it has a way of magnifying every single thing you fear."

"Including monsters hiding in the dark?" he asked lightly.

Cody glowered.

"With beady little eyes and bad breath?"

More glowering.

"Spiked tails and—"

Cody shoved him, and he toppled into the hole—thankfully recovering in time to summon enough magic so he didn't end up shish-kabobbed on the remnants of the stairs.

"Asshole," he called.

Cody just laughed and lowered himself down to the floor, filling the space with violet and emerald magic, lighting up everything from floor to ceiling...including every shadow-filled corner.

They quickly cleared the space, looking for any sign of Rengalla prisoners or casualties.

Often the Dalshie had just killed any Rengalla they came across, but sometimes they'd held them for their version of fun and games (torture, brutality). Because of that and because there were still Rengalla unaccounted for, the LexTals wouldn't stop looking for them.

Starting with the nests and home bases of the Dalshie they knew about.

Then they would continue tracking—money, weapons, sightings—and make certain there weren't any Dalshie left.

That the missing Rengalla weren't cowering in the shadows, unable to escape.

"Nothing," Cody said, after they'd searched every corner, scanned every scrap of paper, gone through every torn notebook and left-behind calendar.

Empty like the previous two they'd checked.

And only...three more to go.

Crammed into two days because they wanted this done, wanted to get home to their mates (and in Cody's case, his baby).

Sighing, because the thought of working through the night wasn't appealing but being away from Darcy for any longer than necessary was even less appealing, so he'd suck it up. He snagged Cody's arm, teleported them both up to the ground floor, and then let him and John take care of the turning rubble to ash part.

He and Mason would save their strength for the next teleport, the next nest.

———

HIS BODY ACHED.

They were on their final search of the final nest.

Two days away from home and they'd found no sign of anything. No Dalshie. No leads on the missing Rengalla.

It was starting to seem that they'd wasted their time.

No clues.

No sign of any bad guys...nor any sign of the good ones.

It was good they'd gotten these locations checked off the list, and he knew they'd needed to do it, but he was hard-pressed to think of it as anything but a waste of time.

Not the best attitude for Dalshie hunting.

And a really shitty one when it came to looking for their missing people.

So, he shoved it down and waited for Cody to finish his call back into base, making sure there wasn't anything else that Tyler and Dante wanted them to check out before they returned.

"Got it," Cody muttered into the cell. "We'll take care of the nest and be back to base by"—he glanced at his watch—"nineteen hundred hours." His eyes flicked to Morgan's, questions in the emerald depths.

Morgan nodded.

It wouldn't take too long to finish this off, and the teleport would only take minutes to get back…just in time to swoop in and save the day by joining in on dinner with his mom. He'd be a little late.

But he'd be there.

Imagining himself riding in on the proverbial white stallion…and reaping all the rewards of Darcy's gratitude later that evening.

He grinned, thinking about all that gratitude and how good it would feel when she repaid it, and began gathering his magic, started directing it toward the building in front of him, nodding when John and Mason joined in, each of them eager to finish this.

Cody hung up the phone, and without a word, his emerald strands joined the collection of other colors, and they set to work reducing the dark place to ash.

The second floor was just collapsing down onto the first when his phone began vibrating.

And then John's.

And Cody's. And Mason's.

With the emergency code.

He cut off his magic, reached into his pocket and yanked out his cell, looking at the screen.

His heart immediately sank, and he saw that the other's faces had gone equally pale.

He started to open his mouth—

And then he felt it.

The bond…it went taut in his mind, that rubber band feeling again…and it snapped.

CHAPTER TWENTY-ONE

Darcy

SHE FROWNED, closed the copy of *Pride and Prejudice*, and scowled.

"Pemberley," she muttered. "His nickname for me is a fucking house."

A large, amazing house, apparently—and one that brought ten thousand pounds a year…but still, a house.

Did that mean he thought she was as *large* as a house?

"Ugh," she grumbled, pushing to her feet and moving to the door.

Her hand was on the knob, and she was turning it, ready to walk the couple of minutes to Morgan's mother's quarters when she looked down at herself.

At what she was wearing.

Jeans and a T-shirt. Worn boots.

"Fuck," she whispered.

She couldn't wear *this*. Matilda was cute and lovely and beautiful and elegant. Darcy couldn't just wear jeans to dinner. She needed to put on a dress and makeup. She needed to…dye her hair or—or—

A knock on the very door she'd been about to walk through.

Since her hand was already on the knob, she turned it, tugged the wooden panel open.

"Hi, honey."

Matilda, in all her elegant, lovely beautifulness, stood in the hallway, a platter in her hands.

"I—"

Darcy panicked.

And…slammed the door. In Matilda's face.

"Oh God. Oh God. *Oh God.*" She yanked at her ponytail. Then realized that she'd slammed the door in Matilda's face.

In. Matilda's. Face.

Fucking hell.

She yanked the door back open, an apology on her tongue. But Matilda didn't allow her to get it out. She merely shifted the platter to one hand, placed her hand on the door, and slowly, inexorably pushed the panel inward.

And followed it in.

Forcing Darcy to step back.

"Hi, honey," Matilda said again, smiling and her voice going warm. She shifted the platter into one hand and gave Darcy a squeeze as she breezed in. "I thought it might be easier if I brought dinner to you. I know you had a shift and must be tired."

"I—"

Matilda dropped her arm and strode down the hall, leaving Darcy sputtering as she watched Morgan's mother begin to unload her platter, setting up plates on Darcy's desk. And silverware. And cloth napkins.

Cloth.

Napkins.

Who used cloth napkins?

Hell, Darcy had half a roll of paper towels that did double duty and sacrificed a roll of toilet paper when it couldn't.

Matilda was totally at ease, not seeming to mind that

Darcy's place was a long way from homey, even with Morgan's additions. In fact, the Colony's decorator only seemed nonplussed when she straightened Darcy's desk chair, glanced around—probably searching for another implement for sitting. But she wasn't thrown for long. A satisfied smile curved her lips as she dragged the bench from the end of the bed (standard to every Rengallan room) over to the desk and patted the cushion.

"Sit, honey," she said, plunking into the desk chair and smoothing a napkin over her lap. Still elegant…just *relaxed* elegant, if that was a thing.

Comfortable in her skin.

Right. That.

While Darcy was ready to crawl out of hers.

Because all of those feelings of not being good enough were circling above her, ready to drop.

Now was the time to say something witty that would put Morgan's mom at ease, assure her that Darcy would be the perfect match for her son and—

"I—" Darcy ran out of steam. After one syllable.

Cool.

Matilda seemed to take pity on her, smiling gently as she patted the cushion again. "I want to hear about your brownies," she said. "I tried one the other day, and they were so delicious that I thought Lex had made them."

"I—" Darcy hesitated again.

And Matilda *definitely* took pity on her, standing, taking Darcy's arm, and physically bringing her to the bench. "But then Lex told me that you had made them," she said, pushing Darcy down, spreading a napkin on her lap, and then pulling out a container of food and passing it over. "And I knew I needed to get the recipe. My boys love chocolate."

And more waiting for Darcy to reply.

And more Darcy feeling like she was fucking this up.

No. She was *definitely* fucking this up.

Matilda seemed nonplussed with the awkwardness, just

pulled out her own container and started eating, giving Darcy time to get her thoughts together.

And, after a moment, she did. Her throat unlocked and she found herself saying, "I...um...I didn't make the recipe." A beat. "It's Lex's. I-I just messed up, actually. I put powdered sugar in instead of flour."

"Powdered sugar?" Matilda's brows rose.

"I know." Darcy bit her lip, managed to get herself together enough to open the lid to the container and followed Matilda's lead by taking a bite. "I don't have a ton of experience baking, or at least not without supervision," she said after she'd chewed and swallowed.

Warm eyes, so much like Morgan's, on hers. "Did you used to bake with your mom?"

Darcy's heart squeezed. "Yes, I did."

A pause. A shadow seeming to cross her face, her expression going conflicted—as though this were now one of the few times she didn't know what she should say. This wasn't elegant or refined, and it finally drew the tension from Darcy's frame.

Then made her forget all about tension at all when Matilda said, "I knew your mom."

Her heart thudded. "You did?"

A nod, those hazel eyes going misty. "We, um, actually grew up together." A smile with a hint of mischief that had Darcy's heart slowing and squeezing. Because it reminded her of Morgan. "And I happen to know that one of her favorite sayings was that accidents in the kitchen are the tastiest mistakes."

She chuckled. "I feel like that could go really wrong."

Matilda grinned. "Yeah, it can. And it does." She nudged Darcy's shoulder, more mischief making itself known. "But in this case, I liked your kitchen accident," she said. "No, I loved it. In fact, it was the best brownie I've had in years."

"Thanks," Darcy whispered.

Matilda's smile softened, and she pulled out another

container, passed it over, and this time it was filled with pasta instead of salad. "Want to try one of *my* kitchen accidents? I didn't have tomato sauce, so I had to use—*gasp*—ketchup."

Darcy chuckled. "How very terrible for you."

Matilda punched her in the shoulder—an inelegant (and quite hard for such a tiny woman) punch. "I should chastise you for your sarcasm. But"—another punch, lighter this time—"sarcasm is my love language, so I'll just join you in it." Her eyes danced with humor and a dash of command (another thing that reminded Darcy of Morgan). "So long as you get me Lex's recipe."

A wink.

Darcy released a breath and took a bite of the confection in front of her, expecting it to be tasty, like the salad had been.

But it wasn't.

It was...not good—*really* not good—but she dutifully managed to choke down her bite.

A fact that Morgan's mom seemed to realize once she'd taken *her* first bite. However, for all her refinement, she didn't manage to keep that bite of pasta down, instead lifting the napkin to her lips and spitting (still somehow daintily...and seriously, come on!) the bite into that cloth napkin.

"Okay, Plan B," Matilda said, snatching the container out of Darcy's lap and plunking it onto the platter, gathering up the remnants of their salads as she said, "We'll go eat in the cafeteria. Then I'll charm the recipe out of Lex, and we'll go back to my place to make a batch of those accident brownies before the boys get home."

"Do you—?" Darcy nibbled at her bottom lip, shook her head.

A hand on her shoulder. "What, honey?"

"I—" *Courage, Darce.* She took a breath, released it slowly. "Do you have any more stories you could tell me about growing up with my mom?" Her eyes slid away. "I just—I just —I miss her."

Silence.

Then gentle fingers gripping hers. "I miss her, too." She slid an arm around Darcy's waist. "And I have *so* many stories, all of which I would be so honored to share with you." A smile. "Over brownies."

Darcy's heart squeezed again. "That sounds—"

It sounded amazing actually, but before she could get that out, the floor started shaking.

"Wh—?" Matilda began.

But Darcy knew what was happening.

She grabbed Matilda's arm, started towing her toward the door, even as the floor rocked and rolled between them. "We have to—"

A huge jerk that knocked them both to their knees.

"Up," she ordered, wrapping an arm around Matilda's waist, hauling her forward.

The candle hit the floor.

The containers and platter joining suit.

The painting fell off the wall, the lamp fell off the bedside table. She towed them down the hall, past the bathroom where bottles of shampoo and conditioner hit the bottom of the shower, where the mirror shattered and went flying.

Almost to the door.

Her fingers grazed the metal knob—

And that was when the world went black.

CHAPTER TWENTY-TWO

Morgan

HE'D STRAINED himself getting them all the way to the Colony, to the shield.

But he didn't give a fuck that his knees were shaking when he pushed through the strands.

Because people were flowing out the front doors of the Colony, gathering on the grass in clumps—not the typical neat lines of an evacuation drill, but rather groupings and clusters of terrified and crying Rengalla, some covered in dust, others in blood.

A few were lying down being treated by the healers.

Where was she?

Where was—

Nowhere on the grass. She had to be helping people. That was what she did.

The ground rolled, sending several of the children out front crying again and nearly knocking him to the grass, especially with his shaking legs. He pushed through the movement, made his way to Dante. "What's the status?"

She had to be inside evacuating people.

"The quake was a big one. We've got trees down everywhere and some destruction in the gardens. A few injuries—broken bones, a couple of head wounds, one panic attack, but Suz has those covered." He glanced down at his tablet. "Most of the Colony is already secure, but we're sweeping to make sure we don't have any risk of collapse, especially since we have some serious structural damage in the old quarters—"

"What?" His heart squeezed. Hard. "Where's Darcy?"

"Everyone's out," Dante said. "I went through and cleared the living quarters myself. Like I said, everything looks intact there, but the engineers are doing a sweep, just to double-check."

"Not *everyone* lives in the new areas. Some—*Darcy*," he gritted, "live in the old quarters. So"—he gripped Dante's shirt—"where the fuck is she?"

Dante's eyes went wide, but he didn't seem to care that Morgan was using him like a rag doll. "Use the bond—"

"I can't *feel* the bond."

"Fuck."

Yeah. Morgan's sentiments exactly.

He dropped his hands, ordered (not giving a shit that he was ordering his boss around), "Do another check. Make sure we're not missing anyone else. I'm going in." He started to round the building.

"Wait," Dante called.

Morgan spun, ready to tell his boss off—and give more fucking orders as needed—but instead of telling him to wait, Dante tossed him an earpiece and a radio. "Take this," he said. "Coms are down. Channel four."

Morgan slipped the earpiece in, changed to channel four.

Then he started running, rounding the building, moving toward the back, toward the older quarters, his mind probing the spot where the bond had gone black, where it had once blazed bright, and where nothing was now residing in its place.

And then he saw the old quarters.

Saw the roof collapsed and the walls in shambles, looking more like a ruin than the abandoned buildings he'd just spent the last two days searching and reducing to ash. Not like the Colony. Not like home. Instead…it was broken.

"Fuck," he hissed, sprinting toward the rubble, hardly aware of Mason next to him, of John and Cody and Tyler and Monroe.

His knuckles split open almost from the moment he began yanking chunks of concrete out of the way, using his magic to stabilize the rest of the space, making sure he didn't have any cave-ins, trying to clear out as much of the debris as quickly as possible.

And…it was never-ending.

And the black, blank feeling in his mind never faded.

The bond was gone.

Darcy was—

"Morgan," Dante's voice jarred him out of his zone, out of his fog of clearing, *clearing* without thinking, without pausing to stop and think and worry and—

"Your mom is also missing."

His brothers went still beside him, and he knew they must have earpieces too, must have realized the same thing he had.

"The dinner," Mason said.

"Fuck." Monroe.

More magic flared, but Morgan was tiring. Could barely summon enough to use it to stabilize where he was digging.

The teleports must have used more energy than he'd realized.

But he had two hands, so he didn't stop digging.

But luckily, he wasn't the only one. They were all digging, all using magic in some capacity, and they were all making progress in clearing out the back side of the Colony, unearthing the emergency exit and the partially collapsed hall.

And, fuck, they were still so far from Darcy's rooms.

So much to dig through.

And she could be dying, and he was here, and—

He reached forward for another rock, hands sliced to shit, and that's when he saw it.

A faint glow of green and brown and gold and—

"There!"

Still nothing in his mind, but there was a gleam, and it was down the corridor toward Darcy's quarters, and—

He shoved, but fuck, his magic was tapped out, and he was feeling woozy. He fell to his knees, feeling the shards of concrete cut into his skin. Hands grabbed at his arms, tried to lift him. But he shook them off, began crawling forward.

"Morg, wait!"

He didn't.

More slices, but he didn't give a shit, not even when he had to squeeze his bulky form through a narrow stretch.

Because there was Bond Magic ahead and that meant—

He turned the corner, head spinning, barely able to keep moving, and he saw it.

Saw her—

On the ground. Unmoving.

Surrounded in a half-sphere of magic, her arm around his unconscious mother, Darcy's body shielding hers. A huge slab of concrete lay across the shield.

And as he watched, as he tried to move closer to get to them both, the strands began to unwind, the magic giving way.

The concrete teetered.

He extended his hand, tried to call forth his powers.

But…he was tapped out.

He had nothing but sparks.

The magic gave way.

The concrete slab fell.

CHAPTER TWENTY-THREE

Darcy

She woke up in the infirmary absolutely tapped out of magic and with a throbbing head.

And scraped palms.

And knees.

And—

"Ouch," she whispered, lifting her hand to her temple, and feeling the scabbed-over wound there.

"Honey."

She blinked, opened her eyes, and saw Matilda was sitting next to her bed, a bruise blooming on her cheek.

"Are you okay?" Darcy asked.

Matilda smiled. "Because of you, honey. You saved us both."

Darcy frowned, trying to remember what had happened. One moment, the world had been shaking. The next, she...

Nothing.

"What happened?"

Matilda sank onto the edge of her bed. "You saved me."

You. Saved. Me.

Three words.

But they brought her right back to that moment, to when she hadn't been able to save another woman, the most important one in her life.

Only...this time was different.

She was okay.

And Darcy was, too.

And—

"Morgan?" she asked, reaching for him instinctively in her mind and finding—

Nothing.

"What happened—where—?"

He wasn't there. Oh God. He wasn't in her mind and—

Matilda gently touched her face, tilting her head so she was looking in the opposite direction, so she could see Morgan sleeping on the bed next to her.

No. Not sleeping.

Unconscious.

"What—"

"He was funneling his magic to you to power the shield around us without being aware of it," Matilda said quietly. "Best Suz thinks is that when you went unconscious, your side of the bond went black. He couldn't feel you, but the bond was still there, still fueling the magic that was protecting you, protecting us."

"Is—is he okay?" she whispered.

"Perfectly fine," Suz said, coming into the room, doing a quick check of Darcy's eyes and ears. "Tapped out, magic-wise, and physically exhausted after the mission and then spending a couple of hours digging you two out." She squeezed Darcy's shoulder. "But he'll be okay."

Darcy released a breath. "He's okay."

"He's okay," Suz reassured her.

Her eyes prickled with tears, and that was when she felt it, felt *him*.

"Don't cry, Pem."

She gasped, tried to hop off the bed to go to him, but he beat her to it, flowing up and over to her in a graceful maneuver that she never could have managed. His arms came around her, and he held her tight.

And though her throat was burning, her eyes filled with tears, she wasn't the one who lost it.

Tears dripped down his face, soaking into the front of her hospital gown. She heard movement and the soft *click* of the door closing and knew Suz and Matilda had gone.

"I'm okay," she whispered. "*We're* okay."

"When you disappeared from my mind..." He shuddered, sniffed. "I—I thought I lost you. We're barely beginning, and I can't lose you, Pem, I *can't*."

"You have me, baby," she whispered. "All of me." A beat. "Even if you teleport off before you hear me declare my undying love for you."

He lifted his head, his eyes slightly reddened. "What?"

She punched him lightly on the shoulder. "You had to be a hotshot, showing off all your cool magical abilities—*pish* teleporting. God, how lame." He laughed, and she felt it in her mind, felt *him* in her mind. Back to normal. His magic returning. Everything stabilizing.

The bond strong. His love—*her* love—strong and out there and safe and warm.

Comfortable.

She didn't have to hide anymore.

He knew it all, wasn't scared of the barbs and open graves, and she was secure enough that he'd seen it all, that he wouldn't turn away from her, even from all the imperfect pieces of her, to not feel like she had to erect those defenses.

Not any longer.

"You love me?" he asked.

"Can't you feel it?"

He froze, but she moved before he did—mentally, anyway— shoving everything she felt for him across the bond, knowing it went through when tears filled his eyes again, and she received love and awe in return.

"You're supposed to be full of snark and lame jokes," she teased, wiping away a tear that escaped.

"You're supposed to be barbed wire and pushing me away."

"Turns out I changed my mind." She snuggled closer. "I kind of like you, Morgan."

He laughed out loud and along the bond. "One of the few."

"Naw."

He waited.

"The *only* one."

An outraged gasp, and then he was tickling her, his warm, roughened, scraped-up hands moving on her body and making her squirm.

And then...making her moan.

"God, I love you," he groaned, pulling her against him and kissing her within an inch of her life. "Thank you for saving my mom."

Her heart squeezed. Hard. "It was nothing."

He cupped her cheek. "It was *everything.*"

Now she was the one ready to cry. But she was done with tears, done with the past and looking back. She wanted the future. *Her* future with the man she loved. "She's wonderful," Darcy whispered. "Almost as wonderful as you."

He got misty-eyed.

"Sap," she teased.

"I swear," he warned. "If you tell the guys..."

"They'll know you're probably whipped by the love of your life."

His lips curved. "Damn right, they will." He kissed her again, his body hard and tempting and making her wish they could teleport back to his rooms, since hers were trashed. "Soon," he said, hearing her thoughts. "As soon as Suz lets us out of here."

"Well, it would probably be sooner if you stopped kissing me."

He pressed a kiss to her jaw. "In a minute." A pause. *"Also, for the record, I'm never letting you out of my sight again."*

She nipped his lips. *"Okay."* A beat as his surprise radiated along the bond. *"But that means you have to come on my night shifts with me."*

He groaned again, but this time it wasn't in pleasure. *"God. No. Not the night shifts."*

"And wash dishes with me," she teased.

"Fine," he grumbled, nibbling her throat. "I'll let you out of my sight. Occasionally."

"Oh, I'm *so* glad I'll have your permission to do my job," she said dryly.

"You're welcome." No regrets with that one.

She laughed and swatted him on the shoulder. "I'd do that harder," she grumbled. "But you look like you're all bruised up."

"I am," he deadpanned, "and I need you to kiss every single one of them. Only you can make it better."

Aw.

But also…snark.

She loved both.

She loved *him*.

"Well," she murmured, pushing him onto his back (with only one near miss of nearly toppling them both out of the hospital bed), and bending to press her lips lightly to his temple. "That's one." His cheek. "Another." His fingers and palms and the backs of his hands. "More." His throat. "Now, are there any more of them?"

His lips curved; his hand went to the button of his jeans—

She smacked it away. "Don't. You. Dare."

He looked up at her with mischief in his hazel eyes and all that mischief directed at her. And love. Along the bond. In his smile. Love and respect and…relief.

That she was okay.

That they were together.

As they were meant to be.

"For the record," she said, snuggling closer. "You need to work on your nickname skills."

A brow lifted.

"You do realize your name for me is a giant, fictional house." A beat. "Which one can surmise means that you view *me* as a giant, fictional house."

His eyes went wide.

He began sputtering. "I—baby—I didn't mean it like that." He cleared his throat. "I just—you can be taciturn and—"

She knew.

She *knew*. And she loved him for it, for the reference and the uniquely Morgan nickname, and…just loved him.

So, she ignored the fact that they were in the narrow hospital bed, that Suz hadn't let them go yet, that they'd had a near miss today, and it could have been devastating if things had gone a little different, and…she kissed him, laughter in her mind, her chest, making the kiss feel as though it were filled with sunshine.

"Never going to live that one down," she murmured, when she'd pulled back, chest heaving.

His fingers brushed her cheek, and he smiled as he said, "God, I hope not."

Her grin matched his, and then she shivered when he nuzzled at her neck. "Because I love nothing more than to make you laugh."

And more sunshine.

And then…she kissed him again.

Because she'd spent too long hiding and wishing that things were different, punishing herself when they weren't.

But no more.

Because it wasn't her fault.

Because she deserved more.

Because she could give Morgan every piece of her and accept every piece of him—good, bad, and in between.

And because they had each other.

They had today.

They had the future.

And it was so much more than she'd ever dared to dream.

Want a free bonus story? Hate missing Elise's new releases?
Love contests, exclusive excerpts and giveaways?

Then signup for Elise's newsletter here!

http://eepurl.com/bdnmEj

And join Elise's fan group, the Fabinators (https://www.
facebook.com/groups/fabinators) for insider information,
sneak peaks at new releases, and fun freebies! Hope to see you
there!

ALSO BY ELISE FABER

Caged

Crashed

Cycled

Breakers Hockey (all stand alone)

Broken

Boldly

Breathless

KTS Series

Riding The Edge

Crossing The Line

Leveling The Field

Scorching The Earth

Love, Action, Camera (all stand alone)

Dotted Line

Action Shot

Close-Up

End Scene

Meet Cute

Love After Midnight (all stand alone)

Rum And Notes

Virgin Daiquiri

On The Rocks

Sex On The Seats

Life Sucks Series (all stand alone)

Train Wreck

Hot Mess

Dumpster Fire

Clusterf*@k

FUBAR

Roosevelt Ranch Series **(all stand alone, series complete)**

Disaster at Roosevelt Ranch

Heartbreak at Roosevelt Ranch

Collision at Roosevelt Ranch

Regret at Roosevelt Ranch

Desire at Roosevelt Ranch

Phoenix Series **(read in order)**

Phoenix Rising

Dark Phoenix

Phoenix Freed

Phoenix: LexTal Chronicles **(rereleasing soon, stand alone, Phoenix world)**

From Ashes

In Flames

To Smoke

ABOUT THE AUTHOR

USA Today bestselling author, Elise Faber, loves chocolate, Star Wars, Harry Potter, and hockey (the order depending on the day and how well her team -- the Sharks! -- are playing). She and her husband also play as much hockey as they can squeeze into their schedules, so much so that their typical date night is spent on the ice. Elise changes her hair color more often than some people change their socks, loves sparkly things, and is the mom to two exuberant boys. She lives in Northern California. Connect with her in her Facebook group, the Fabinators or find more information about her books at www.elisefaber.com.

facebook.com/elisefaberauthor

amazon.com/author/elisefaber

bookbub.com/profile/elise-faber

instagram.com/elisefaber

goodreads.com/elisefaber

pinterest.com/elisefaberwrite

tiktok.com/@elisefaberauthor